Chasing

Dreams

Tales of a Travelling
Fisherman

Jeremy Norris

ISBN: 978-1-4251-9033-0

 www.trafford.com

North America & international
toll-free: 1 888 232 4444 (USA & Canada)
phone: 250 383 6864 ♦ fax: 812 355 4082

Dedication.

For my family and to all fishermen
who chase their dreams.

Contents.

The traveller fancies he has seen the country. So he has, the outside of it at least; but the angler only sees the inside. The angler only is brought close, face to face with the flower and bird and insect life of the rich river banks, the only part of the landscape where the hand of man has never interfered.

- Charles Kingsley, 1890.

eturning home from New Zealand utterly broke was no fun! My friends and family thought I had done my thing and that I was now ready to move on; they were wrong, it was what I wanted to do for the rest of my life. My divorced mother grew up in a council house, had little money and had to bring four boys up alone. What a nightmare it must have been for her. But somehow she managed it.

I'd drunk with my grandfather for years. He was a friend and when times were hard he was always there. I would sit around Somerset cider bars and began to realise how the world worked, and for me at least, it wasn't about money. Most people work all their lives in the hope of following their dreams but my grandfather had made me realise that others were sometimes mistaken. He had taught me a lot.

My brother Peter had drunk with him while I was travelling. Like me, he knew him. His cider wasn't going down well, he was ill. After he had died and been buried his grave was covered in wild flowers. I didn't go to the funeral as we had made a pact.

"Write things down," my grandmother once told me, "otherwise you will forget." I bought a cheap notepad without lines as, like my mother, I hate lined paper. I decided to keep a diary of my travels. Someone once said keep a diary and one day it will keep you. I think it's probably true.

Chapter 1.

Los Roques, Venezuela.

$\mathcal{B}$onefishing is the very art and finesse of fishing. Imagine the fish, the people, the amazing scenery and you're in the Caribbean, a complete visual assault on your senses. All fly fishermen should go at least once in their fishing career, get a suntan, see the wildlife, and feel the power of a hooked bonefish with the line hissing as it tears off across the flats in some of the most untouched and beautiful places on the planet. I didn't know it then but I do now, and I'm glad I grabbed life by its throat and took my chance.

I saved whatever money I could, scrounging food to survive and walking the local trout river each day to try to maintain some kind of sanity. The sad thing is that the trout river I knew is gone, like so many English trout streams it has been abused and left to rot. I turned up at Heathrow airport ten months later feeling quite mad preparing to fly off to Caracas Venezuela to try to catch a bonefish! I'd only seen an obscure video of the place. I flew to Caracas as green as grass with no command of the Spanish language.

On landing I took a taxi as the drivers warned I would get shot if I waited for the local bus. I was later to find out it was just a scare tactic. I wanted to stay for three months so every penny was needed if I was to survive. I made it down the coast and found a cheap hotel. That night, I asked for a beer but the barman just looked blank at me, he clearly didn't understand English. I knew from that point on it was going to be tough going and things weren't helped by my feeling weird from the long flight. Was I mad? What the hell was I doing here? With so little money for me to live on, I'd taken a real gamble.

I kept reminding myself daily that bonefish on a fly was the reason! I slept. Morning came and stupidly I hitched back to the airport, before taking a bus into Caracas to try and find out some information. Caracas is best described as organised chaos, always something new to see but very dangerous. It was extremely hot and this was made worse by me having to carry a huge backpack.

I finally made it to the tourist office, which was on the top floor of one of the two tallest buildings in the city. There, I waited outside the office until finally a lady turned up; she smiled and beckoned me in. It turned out to be a waste of time as she didn't speak any English and just handed me a couple of brochures, again in Spanish. I thanked her then left to find a bus back to the airport. On arriving at the domestic terminal I found out that there were no available flights to the islands until the next day. I waited for a local bus and returned to my hotel before crashing out, exhausted by the heat and my backpack. I had been chasing my tail.

The next day I again took a bus back to the airport and found a local who could speak broken English to translate for me. Next I found myself on a four-seater flying out to the archipelago of Los Roques sixty miles off the coast; it had been a mad journey. Gazing through the window of the plane made me feel slightly uneasy as I wondered what was out there waiting for me.

It was about half an hour before I saw the outer reaches of the islands and found myself gobsmacked! As the plane approached I gazed out in wonder while glancing to look at the other people sitting around me; their faces were lit up bright blue from the reflection of the water. It was spectacular. Island after island were surrounded by flats and it looked to me like bonefishing heaven.

The plane began to circle the main island, Grande Roque, and swept in for the landing. It was a seat of your pants landing on the tiny runway until finally the plane ground to a halt and engines were cut. I had arrived. They unloaded my backpack and rods from the nose of the aircraft and I crossed the tarmac.

3

After I had spent a while looking at the pelican's diving on the baitfish, I found the terminal was a hut, nothing more. I paid the fees to enter the national park then walked to find a suitable place to camp.

With the backpack lying heavily on my back I entered the town. No roads, no cars, just posadas, and the sand, just how I like it. The archipelago consists of over three hundred islands, almost one for every day of the year and flying in to see the magnificence of them for the very first time filled my heart with excitement. It was heaven on earth. I walked through the sandy roads, passing brightly coloured posadas, watching fishermen preparing long lines for the evening. Eventually, I found the inparque's office to try to get a camping permit. It was hand signals, gesturing in the most effective way possible; anything to make myself understood, as I had no Spanish and they had no English.

After an hour of red tape I managed to get all the permits necessary to fish and camp. That night in the local bar, stressed out after the ordeal, I sat drinking a cold beer knowing I had to keep going as the bonefish were waiting. The next day after a sleepless night on the beach I found the local shop and bought breakfast and water, enough to last me two weeks as the outer keys had no running water. I sat by my tent watching the pelican's engaged in their daily assault on the baitfish. Like them, I needed to fish, but how was I going to get a lift? This happened purely by chance. A friendly Swiss guy turned up who just happened to speak English. He also offered me a lift on his yacht to one of the outer keys. It was a real stroke of luck and I grabbed it with both hands. He turned up an hour later on the beach in his tender, helped me load up supplies and we left to find his yacht. As we headed out to sea I felt excited. What would I find? The sun was out, the sea calm and it was blissful under sail. Then, to help me cool down a little I was handed a cold beer.

We crossed the channel for about an hour or so until a tiny key started to appear. Then we entered the lea of the island and as we did so I gazed in disbelief because the whole lagoon was exploding with fish, crashing on baitfish! I had found a very special place. The water was so clear it resembled a giant swimming pool. He dropped me off on the shore then I unloaded my gear, thanked him then he left and moored up.

I felt lonely after he had left me and my pile of supplies on the shore. When I had caught my breath I left the whole lot on the beach and wandered off to find a suitable place to camp. It was not long before

I found the perfect spot; the only palm tree on the island and shade, a welcome escape from the sun, which was blistering hot. Three journeys of lugging gear up the beach followed leaving me covered in sweat. I lay in the shade of the palm tree recovering having found solace.

After finally recovering I embarked upon the task of making camp. It took most of the afternoon. When evening came the sun started to disappear and with it the heat. I was established.

Bonefish camp under the palm tree.

I sat alone, quiet, the gentle breeze of the Caribbean, soothing my soul and feeling good but if truth be told I missed my grandfather. Nevertheless, I thought of him that afternoon. I boiled water on the tiny petrol stove using fuel blagged from the local fishermen and made some black coffee. They knew that like themselves I was poor, so they gave it to me willingly.

As I walked along the beach the stars were glistening brightly as there were no lights for miles. The stars seemed to touch the horizon and create the impression of a dome. I remembered Zimbabwe and how free I had felt for just two weeks of my life that night and had the same feeling only this time the feeling was enhanced by the fact that I had found such an amazing place and although I had little money at least time was on my side.

First there was the sound of a generator, then lights; I saw a fisherman and his family in a place by the shore. They greeted me kindly, with hand signals and in awful Spanish I tried asking for a meal. Somehow I was able to make them understand. I didn't know it then but it was the local fishermen's restaurant and I was its only client. I waited for my food at a table lit by a single candle.

There were no carpets, just the beach between

Los Roques fisherman.

my toes; a part of the place. The fisherman, tired and half asleep from the heat of the day, lay in a hammock but as ever he was keeping a watchful eye on a green as grass English bonefisherman. Sleep came easily that night for once the sound of the sea lapping on the shore and the rustle of the palm tree above I felt at peace.

I awoke early the next day feeling refreshed and heard the sound of the pelican's screeching as they dived onto the baitfish. I hastily made a black coffee, grabbed my fishing gear then walked off down the shore to talk to the local fishermen and hopefully secure a lift to the bonefish flats. On walking down the beach I found out they had left to check their long lines so I continued to the point of the island.

I walked along the beach and gazed at the crystal clear water in search of bonefish. As ever, the pelican's were diving on the baitfish. Off the shore, between the yachts, black tern's screeched as they followed a school of yellowtail, flying close to the surface. They were working as a team with the fish as they chased baitfish to the surface. More birds could be seen further out, following blue runners in the hope of a meal. Even though I was an experienced fisherman I watched on in wonder.

I had noticed a flat on the point of the island; the

previous day we had passed it on the yacht and it had looked a likely spot for bonefish. When I arrived there I couldn't see any fish, the water was only ankle deep, but I decided to wade in anyway. As I did so, I cast a fly on a floating line on a 14lb leader in search of a bonefish. On about the fourth cast, while stripping the fly back, everything went solid. I had struck, I had found a fish. Whatever was attached made the line hiss as it raced across the flat from left to right into deeper water. The power was immense. I hadn't seen the fish take but felt it must be a bonefish so I piled on the pressure. Three times it went into the backing until finally it began to tire and a silver fin and tail came into focus in the shallow water - my first bonefish. I led it on to the shore, dropped the fly rod and pounced on it. I held it in my hands and was astounded by its beauty; it had a bright green back and an armoury of bright, silver, mirror-like scales.

I quickly took a photograph of the fish before reviving it and then letting it swim away. As it did dematerializing in the bright blue water just six feet in front of me, it was a magic moment. I stood trembling as I knew I had found what I had so desperately sought. In hope of another bonefish I fished on to no avail. It was mid morning and I left the flat walking again down the shore in hope of finding a lift. At the fishermen's restaurant I bumped into the Swiss guy who had given me a lift. I told him of my catch. "This afternoon I'll drop you off over there", he pointed to a key about a mile or so away. "There's loads of bonefish there". I arranged to meet him later and then made it back to camp to rest.

Captured bonefish.

The heat began to subside at around 3.00pm. It had been blistering. Once again I walked down to the shore to meet up with the Swiss guy. I found him in the fishermen's restaurant. His tender was on the shore so we climbed aboard then sped off. It didn't take longer than fifteen minutes or so to cross the channel to the key he had pointed out to me earlier. I watched as he left me alone on the shore, unsure as to what I would find. Before he left he arranged to pick me up in a couple of hours. The tiny key felt desolate, untouched by man, and one thing I immediately noticed was the huge flat which lay in front of it. Instantly I began to spot bonefish in the knee-deep water. They were everywhere, going about their daily business of hunting baitfish, shrimps and crabs. I didn't wade in at first but crept about the shore, crouched down out of their field of vision. That was a trick I had learned from my uncles as a boy when I hunted trout with worms.

I cast a fly at one of the bonefish. It followed. I sped up the retrieve, twitched the fly then it pounced on it. It raced off then the fly line tore down the flat, with the reel emptying deep into the backing as I tried in vain to take control. It just ran and ran. On a lose clutch it snapped the 14lb leader as the run became ferocious. I was staggered.

When I regained my composure I set up again as I could see more bonefish. As a group of them came through the flat I made ready and this time I was ankle deep in water. I cast at the lead fish, one which peeled off, speeded up and grabbed the fly. As I struck and as it ran I held the rod high above my head, giving the fly line a chance to avoid the coral.

A bonefish gets released to fight another day.

As the bonefish raced off I loosened the clutch to let the fish run and what a run! The plan worked and the bonefish briefly stopped. I checked it and managed to turn it but still it made two more monster runs well into the backing before it began to circle me. By now it was tiring and I finally had it in my possession. I held my prize, a 5lb bonefish. Now I knew what all the fuss was about. These fish were quite staggering; their beauty, power, and fighting abilities were wonderful.

I gazed at the fish in wonder and took a photo before it returned into the flats where it belonged; it was a special moment indeed.

That afternoon I landed five bonefish and got snapped off by more, just by the sheer ferocity by which they ran. I got picked up later and as we crossed the channel I told the Swiss guy about my catch. He dropped me off on the beach at camp under the palm tree before we said our goodbyes as he was to leave the next day. I lay quiet, thinking of the day's fishing in the shade of the palm tree, it had been astounding. As the light began to fade I put on my shortwave radio and as the first star began to appear I listened to Big Ben chime on the BBC World Service. I felt content.

Afterwards I walked down the shore to the fishermen's restaurant and as ever they greeted me with a warm welcome. I sat alone writing my diary by candlelight. That day, I felt I had achieved something. I waited for my evening meal of fresh fried cero (Spanish mackerel), rice and coleslaw. The fish had been caught that very day by Andreas the fisherman who owned the restaurant. I had watched him carefully as he moored up his small wooden boat just off the shore. Using a hand line with wire trace, he hooked on a single live sardine, and as he threw it over the side, scooped a few more out of the live well which he kept in the middle of his boat and threw them in to entice the fish to feed. He was an expert, making me feel like an apprentice, he had a lifetime of experience and of course it tasted exquisite. Totally satisfied I walked back to camp and gazed at the stars, the evening was balmy. That night I slept well.

I awoke at first light, my first job of the day a morning swim. Then I boiled water for a black coffee and while I waited I smothered myself in sun cream, a daily chore I loathed, but it was essential otherwise I'd have cooked. Fishing gear was ready prepared before turning in for the night. I left camp in search of a lift to the key I fished the previous day.

It was another perfect day with light winds and not a cloud to be seen, perfect conditions in which to sight fish for bonefish. I was excited by the prospect.

Luck was on my side and I paid a local fisherman for a boat ride. Another amazing day's fishing was to follow. I found a small school of bonefish tailing in the seagrass. With baited breath I cast the fly, a tail disappeared and one went after the

Bonefish on seagrass.

fly with half its back out of the water. It grabbed the fly, I struck and it exploded in the shallow water. Then it sped off, the rest of the school scattered, the reel screamed and line tore from the spool deep into the backing, I chased the fish across the seagrass, it was making for the deep water, I managed, rod above head to turn it and after an epic battle with the bonefish going deep into the backing another four times I led the fish up on the shore and finally held my prize. I briefly held the fish, took a photo and it swam off, slowly at first then quicker as it regained its strength. Amazing. Even more so when you consider their power even after the experience of the previous day I still had bonefish snap 14lb line, it was mind blowing. But still I ended the day with bonefish; caught, photographed and released.

9th October 1998.

Fished from 9.00am-2.00pm and caught four bonefish; the first two 4lb the second two nearer the 5lb mark. Heat today, as every day here, blistering. This is such a beautiful place but it's also a very harsh environment in which to live and really takes it out of you! As expected, each bonefish fought incredibly hard.

Los Roques, Venezuela.

Every time I hold one of these fish in my hands I feel a joy, which is hard to put into words.

That evening in camp I sat under the palm tree and realised my legs had caught the ferocity of the sun and as the light began to fade the pain got worse and worse. I kept reassuring myself I was being soft but my legs were bright red, my skin tight and they were beginning to swell. I was in some sorry state and it hurt badly. I walked down to the beach for supper. (I didn't feel like food but knew I must eat.) Afterwards, under candlelight, I gazed out to see a light in the darkness. It began to get closer and closer until I could make out the unmistakable sound of an outboard motor. The boat pulled up on the shore revealing a boat full of men. I was amazed as five Americans and a local fisherman laden with gear unloaded the boat and walked into the restaurant. I got up to greet them; like me they were fly fishermen. I shook their hands. One of them looked down at my legs and said, "You poor chap" and without saying a word they all emptied their bags and looked for first aid kits. Among their medical supplies they had creams and ointments for sunburn. As we talked I rubbed them in to soothe the pain. If they hadn't turned up I would have been in big

18

trouble.

That night as we drank beer I told them stories of my fishing exploits, I think they understood what I was about and respected me for it. Later I staggered back, my legs swollen from the sun and I lay in bed, in pain and suffering. I felt low and ill. I couldn't sleep, the pain was horrible and the night heat accentuated it. I drifted off to sleep, an hour later.

After a restless night I awoke in pain with my legs burning. I made a black coffee and somehow it didn't taste the same as usual. I walked down to the shore and met the Americans; they were off to fish the flats. They invited me but I was in too much pain. One of them, Peter, stayed behind. I later found out he was an Englishman who had gone to the states in the sixties to customise cars and ended up living there. He knew I was in trouble so he'd decided to stay with me and fish for bonefish along the shore. I fished in army socks and trousers to protect me from the sun. No fish was caught that day and I returned to camp with blistered feet - the socks had rubbed! I slept in pain, it was awful.

I awoke the next day again after a sleepless night; my legs felt a little easier but still they burned. I kept the sun off them but that day I fished with the heat continuing to aggravate the pain. I knew I had to keep going, after all it was all I could do in the circumstances so I just put on a brave face.

After three days of suffering I awoke to find the pain in my legs had eased, partly due to the creams the Americans had given me, which I rubbed in constantly. The swelling had gone down; it was a huge relief. One thing was certain: I had underestimated the sun. Now feeling much better, I took a deep breath and carried on as though nothing had happened. Peter stayed with me as the others went off to fish the flats. He had long hair, a beard, a kind face and reminded me of each of my uncles who had taught me to fish. Peter and I got on instantly. I took him to the flat where I had caught my first fish he cast a few times and snapped his rod, I felt for him. The others, on returning, lent him a rod for the next day's fishing but I knew it was little consolation for him. I knew he felt bad without his own rod, I tried to console him but knew he felt like a spectator. At that time I myself didn't have a backup rod I decided there and then I must always carry one!

For the rest of our time together Peter and I fished while the rest of the group sped around in search of bonefish. We concentrated on the small key nearby and ended up catching more bonefish, and good ones at that. One evening we were sitting together as the others talked and I suggested to Peter we take a walk up the beach. He agreed. We grabbed our spinning rods. As we walked along we talked about the day's fishing; it was a lovely evening, the coral sand between our toes looked pink, the sea midnight blue. As the sun began to set I noticed a commotion far up the beach. The pelican's were frantically diving on the baitfish. A large school of fish were beneath them and I ran while urging Peter to follow. When we arrived at the feeding frenzy I could see large jacks going mad; they had herded the baitfish to the shore where there was no escape, binging on them. The pelican's and tern's screeched out as they picked up the scraps. Then they would disperse back to the deep and regroup before the whole process would start again.

I watched the birds closely following the school overhead. They came again, crashing and porpoising through the baitfish; they were everywhere. I cast and instantly hooked up while Peter caught up. "Cast!" I shouted, and I saw his rod bolt over, we were both into fish. Our reels emptied as the hooked fish followed the school. We both ran up and down the shoreline barefooted, trying to keep control of the fish but they were too strong for us.

"It's gone!" cried Peter. He'd lost his. Mine was still on and after a scrap and a half I landed what turned out to be a horse-eyed jack, well over 15lb. I quickly killed the fish and started to run again. I cried out to Peter to follow the school, which was by now a long way down the shore. We were determined not to be beaten and managed to catch up with the fast-moving shoal. We got in front of them and I hooked up another but Peter didn't connect. My rod jarred over the reel screamed in protest as the horse-eyed jack ran heading again for the deep. I piled on the pressure and managed to turn it. Peter watched on as I fought the powerful fish but eventually luck was again on my side and I beached it. A carbon copy of the first fish.

By now it was nearly dark so we returned back to camp carrying the fish. "Caught anything?" was the first question. We held them up. They all looked shell-shocked, but they handed us beers and smiled. The fish went to the Andreas (the restaurant owner) as a gift for he had been so friendly and hospitable to us all.

A couple of days later it was time to leave and I was sad to go. Andreas took us all back to the main island. The Americans left for the mainland that evening, while I flew the next day. I was sitting alone in the bar that evening, drinking beer and reflecting on the fishing. It had been unbelievable, true bonefishing heaven. I had caught over forty bonefish.

Los Roques bonefish.

After the bonefishing I returned to the mainland and took the local bus into Caracas. As a boy gazing at the TV (which was as boring as ever) I recalled something that was worth watching but it had been many years ago. A programme of a boat, a dugout canoe, with an outboard motor going against the current up a river surrounded by rainforest. As they passed a bend in the river the camera began to scan, higher and higher, up into the clouds until finally it stopped revealing a ribbon of water, a waterfall. Salto Angel, the Angel Falls of Venezuela. That day I promised myself one day I would see it. I kept my promise to myself. As a man with a boyhood dream I left the airport by local bus to Caracas to chase my dream.

I was dropped off at the tube station and was surprised to find it clean, making London's underground look grimy. With a sun-kissed body, shorts and army Burgen backpack I must have looked a sight to the people dressed in suits going to work. I was in the city to work out a way by bus to the interior of the country and to see the Angel Falls. Things got very dangerous in one of the local bus stations. One guy distracted me with his newspaper, another shouted, while a small rat-like guy grabbed all my money out of the leg pocket of my army trousers. Instinctively I fell on him, the backpack and I pinning him against the floor. I got up and put my British army boot across his neck and snatched my money back. Somehow he squirmed free and got lost in the crowd. I scrambled onto a bus and fled back to the coast and a cheap hotel to gain some kind of composure. I had been lucky.

Determined not to fail at the last hurdle I again returned to the hustle and bustle of Caracas. But after the events of the previous day my guard was up. It was late afternoon before I had sorted things out. Although I had little money I found a whorehouse (love hotel) and booked a room. These love hotels double as cheap hotels. As I climbed the stairs a girl passed by, smiling, looking for business, in her no-doubt drugged up stupor. I entered the room where I found Raoul, a Dutch journalist. We instantly got on and it was just as well as there was just one double bed and mirrors on the ceiling. We left and went to eat in the Chinese over the road and after a few beers we left and slept, both of us clutching our sleeping bags against our necks.

The next morning I discovered over breakfast that he too was on a mission to see the Angel Falls. So after coffee we left for the coach station. It was good to have back up and a lot safer. The coach journey was to the city of Ciudad Bolivar. It was an arduous journey made worse by the air conditioning, we arrived feeling bitterly cold. It had taken ten hours. We again shared a room a cheap dive but at least it had a balcony that overlooked the Orinoco River. It was dark and later we had a few beers before going to sleep.

Over the next day we arranged a cheap way of getting to Canaima, the gate way to the falls. From there it was an eight-hour boat ride up river to the base camp. After asking around - or at least after Raoul who spoke Spanish had asked around - we booked a trip. The first stage was a seat of your pants ride on a four-seater aeroplane. The next day was exciting: we were dropped off by taxi at the tiny local airport. Jimmie Angel's plane stood as a monument outside, the American who had discovered the falls by chance and how it got it's name. After the usual chaos associated with airports we were finally airborne. We could see below us the jungle and we swept up the river until finally we landed at Canaima. That night we slept with a local family in hammocks and I awoke on the floor as it was more comfortable. On the first day, we were taken to a nearby waterfall, Salto el Sapo, an amazing spectacle. A path led behind it and a walk through it revealed the thundering water in front. It was amazing. Again we finished the day with a beer or two. The next day we awoke in a state of excitement - it was time to travel by dugout canoe to finally come face-to-face with the Angel Falls.

At 997 metres the falls stands majestically among tepuies and rainforest; the highest waterfall

Salto Angel, the Angel Falls of Venezuela.

in the world, discovered by chance by Jimmie Angel, an American who landed in his four-seater on the marshy surface in search of gold at the top of one of the largest tepuis named Auyantepui (mountain of God) in 1937. He couldn't take off. Eleven days later after an arduous trek he and his wife and two companions emerged from the dense jungle to tell of their discovery. Like the TV programme from years before I passed the same bend in the river and there it was in all its glory. I slept in a hammock at the base camp, and for three days I saw her in all her moods as I crossed the river daily and clambered through the jungle for about an hour to bathe in the huge pool at the base of the falls and gaze at the amazing waterfall.

I swam to the bottom and took a single stone, which on returning to England I handed to my brother Paul, a sculptor. A few weeks later he gave it back to me, now carved. I returned home feeling as light as a feather and as fit as a flea having blown away a few cobwebs!

Chapter 2.

Belize, Central America.

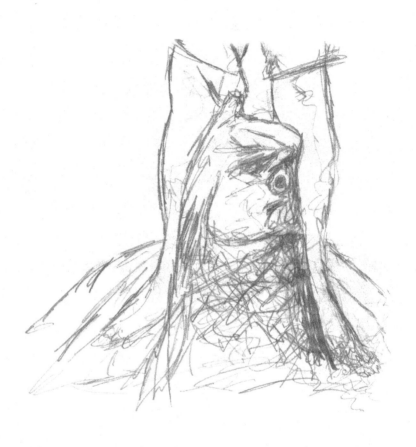

$\mathcal{T}$he first time I met David was on a tiny island off the Belizian coast and part of the Glovers Atoll. The huge Barrier Reef is the second largest in the world with only the Great Barrier Reef in Australia being bigger. I'd been roughing it and had ended up in a wooden shack waiting for the boat to take me out to the island. It was a weird place and I spent two days there, my only company being scorpions and lizards, which crept up the walls and the ceiling; I watched them in the candlelight before drifting off to sleep. A walk to another shack to buy beer and food made the evenings bearable. Walking up the dusty track following the river left me feeling strangely alone, but somehow it felt good and I felt free. The walk was long but I kept going in the twilight until lights and buildings started to appear and I was able to visit the shop and buy some bottles of beer.

The next morning brought the unmistakable sounds of the jungle I heard a noise becoming until I realised it was an outboard motor, the boat. It was a relief. I saw it coming up the river and soon it was tied up on the shore. Out clambered a Belizian guy and we shook hands before going off together to buy supplies. On returning we loaded up and left for the island. The river was wonderful. Howler monkeys shouted from the jungle as we left the river mouth and headed out into the blue of the Caribbean Sea. The ride became sloppy and was a surprisingly long journey but eventually a tiny island started to appear on the horizon. It was sheltered from the wind and as we entered to the lea of the island a huge blue lagoon started to appear; coral sand lined the shore; there were palm trees for shade, seemingly untouched by man.

The woman who owned the island was an American and looked as though she had become a native, her skin leathery from the sun. She met me on the shore where I greeted her and told her I was a fisherman. "Then you need to meet David," she replied, "he's one as well." I knew I'd come to the right place.

I was shown around the island, it didn't take very long as it was so small. I could camp there, but there were so many sand flies I decided to take a beach hut, cheap at $99 for the week. It was a typical beachcomber's hut: simple with an oil cooker, single candle and a bed along with a mosquito net. Simple but idyllic. It was set on stilts to escape the sand flies. I settled in.

I met David (an American) on the shore and

discovered he had a hut there. I introduced myself then we sat and talked bonefishing as we looked over the aqua marine of the lagoon. He had a glint in his eye as he spoke and I could tell he had seen life. A plan was agreed upon, namely, to meet up in the morning and go and wade the huge lagoon which surrounded the island in search of bonefish. When morning came David greeted me, climbing up the steps to my hut and clasping a fresh pot of black coffee. It was a very good way to start the day.

Beachcomber's hut.

As ever, it had been a struggle to get here, working

with my brother Peter as a dogsbody for low pay, but I had somehow managed to save enough money for a planned three-month trip chasing tarpon. Just before I left, Peter told me of an American Airstream trailer. He knew I had always wanted one and it was a rarity indeed to turn up in Somerset, England.

I was undecided as to whether to fish or try to buy it so I asked Peter for advice. His answer was to go catch the tarpon, return home and get the Airstream. It might be still there. He said it with a smile on his face as he knew it was what I needed to hear. I wanted to fish. I left England on a mission to hunt tarpon, having planned to fly to Florida take the Greyhound bus down to the Florida Keys and fish three days with a guide. Then I hoped to spend ten days or so in the country, before flying to Belize in Central America where I would rough it and fish. I promised myself before leaving I wasn't going to come home until I had caught a tarpon and a giant one at that.

Guides in the Keys were expensive, $375 a day, but I knew it was a good investment as that was the best way to learn. It was May, prime time in the keys for the giant tarpon to appear. I got off the Greyhound bus at Big Pine Key and made for the camping ground. I turned up at the gates with my backpack. "Here's a key for the gate", the guy said.

"Don't have a car," I replied.

"You'd still better take one, just in case."

I refused, he just couldn't comprehend I didn't have a car. This was because everyone in the States has one. As it happened, I entered the camping ground feeling good that I didn't have one! Big Pine Key is famous because out in the front of this tiny island lays a huge flat Bahia Honda, world famous for giant tarpon, which they patrol.

As expected, the camping ground was sterile but at least it was okay on the seashore. It also was next to the highway and close to one of the many bridges that links the Florida Keys together. I found a camping spot and set up camp as far away from people as I could. It was getting dark so I lay down and slept. The ground was hard and made for a sleepless night and I awoke heavy eyed. I sat quietly and watched the ocean, finally I had made it! The hunt for a giant tarpon was on and it felt very good.

The first thing I did after a black coffee that morning was ring the guide. I had chosen him because back in England I had e-mailed all the top guides in the Keys and decided the guide who responded the quickest would get the job. I was pleased that he was French and I liked the fact that

---

he must love his fishing to be in the Keys so far away from home chasing the tarpon. I rang him and arranged to meet him in the morning. This was convenient for him as he could just turn up in his flats boat as the camping ground had its own dock. I awoke to stormy clouds with no sign of the sun. I was sight fishing so I felt downhearted when the guide turned up. I suggested waiting until the next day, he told me that conditions was fine. Of course, at $375 a day he would say that. He didn't turn up in his boat, and instead appeared in a four-wheel drive. We got in and drove off to find his boat down the coast; I knew it was a sign of the bad weather.

It was businesslike, with no banter; when we turned up at his 14ft flats boat, we got aboard, started the engine, and powered off to find a sheltered lagoon among the mangroves. When the boat stopped, the guide asked me to cast for a while. So as instructed I picked up a fly rod and began to cast. He looked on in silence, he was testing my skill. He grunted a few times as if to say he'll do and then started the engine before we left to find the fish. The flats boat slammed on the waves as we powered through the sea. Eventually, though, after a very rough ride we arrived at the flats. The sun came out briefly; we were being chased buy the storm, dark clouds loomed threateningly behind us. The engine was cut and I was handed a Sage ten weight fly rod. I felt nervous. He anchored up and we waited for the tarpon to appear on the flat. The water was gin clear. The reflections of the sky in the water on the flats were lit up by the sun while the balmy breeze covered my body. I tingled with anticipation. The guide spotted the first tarpon from his platform. "Two o'clock" he shouted, but I didn't see it. I cast blindly in hope, but it was gone as quickly as it had appeared. The clouds again blocked the sun as the storm approached, making sight fishing impossible. The guide pretended it wasn't a problem, I knew it was! With the approaching storm we just chased our tail all day. We ended the first day with me frustrated, the guide had tried pulling the wool over my eyes and I wasn't too impressed. Needless to say I returned back to camp fishless.

That night I was restless, I only had two days left. I needed good weather and I could only hope it would improve overnight, but it felt hopeless.

I poked my head out of the tent in the morning; the sun was just coming up and with it clear blue skies. The storm clouds had passed overnight, I couldn't believe it. I got ready to fish, this time with fire in my belly, as I knew the hunt for tarpon was on. The guide turned up on time, this time in the boat at the camping ground dock. Like me, he knew conditions were perfect. I climbed aboard grasping a black coffee and we sped off. We didn't talk much as words were not needed, the tarpon awaited us. Ten minutes after leaving the guide cut the engine, he had spotted fish and it was tarpon. He pointed. My eyes nearly popped out of my head when I spotted them. I could see huge fish - the guide estimated the smallest to be 80lb, the rest of the school a whole lot bigger - and they were daisy-chaining. This is when they form a circle and porpoise in and out of the water, head to tail. Not a lot is known about why they do this but for any fisherman it makes the hair stand up on the back of the neck.

He handed me the rod as he poled me close to the fish. With rod in one hand and fly in the other I was ready. "Now!" he said. I cast, slowly at first then speeded up. The fly landed in the middle of the school. I stripped it back. Nothing. Again I cast to them with the same result. I then cast the fly but this time it landed perfectly just in front of one of the circling fish. I stripped the fly back then it stopped. Then I struck. Out of the marine blue a huge tarpon leapt, gills flaring, with its armoury of silver scales lit up by the morning sun, then abruptly threw the

Leaping tarpon.

hook! The guide looked at me and said, "That's what we call a hook up." I was stunned.

We continued to chase the school until they disappeared, still daisy-chaining as they moved downtide. I had cast until my arms burned, but it was no use as they had been spooked. When they had left, the guide told me how I had made the boat wobble. "I nearly fell off my poling platform, you need casting instruction."

"I hooked one, didn't I?" I replied. We continued to search for tarpon while the guide poled us across the flats. As we drifted we watched the marine life, lit up by the glistening water. A school of spotted eagle rays passed beneath the boat and their beauty astounded me.

With no tarpon showing it was time for casting instruction. I thought I was doing well until I was shown the error of my ways. We communicated properly for the first time and in those two hours he taught me how to cast. I took it in.

One day that knowledge came into its own. A bonefish lay tailing in a lagoon but I couldn't reach it. I had stalked it for about twenty minutes in the hope of getting a shot but didn't dare to get any closer as it would surely have been spooked. I knew if the cast wasn't perfect my chance would be gone.

My heart pounded as I remembered what the guide had passed on to me. I set up my cast and threw out a perfect line, the fly landed just six inches in front of the bonefish. With that the tail disappeared and I nailed it! I remember as it sped away the hairs on the back off my neck pricking up. It was one of those memories no fly fisherman ever forgets.

We left the shelter of the shore and once again sped off to find new flats. The tide was running again and and we knew it was time for the tarpon to appear. The engines were cut and we staked out a huge flat close to one of the bridges. Expectations were high when we spotted tarpon, but they were too far away from us. We waited a little longer then they came. "Fish!" the guide shouted. There was a school of maybe fifty tarpon. Soon they were upon us and I cast at the leading fish. I expected an instant take but there was nothing so I cast again. There were so many tarpon how could I fail? The school had nearly gone, having refused all my offerings but then I frantically cast to the last group of fish. I saw a tarpon peel off and grab the fly; I struck it and the rod jarred over as a hooked tarpon powered off following the school the line emptying from the spool deep into the backing then the line went limp.

It had spat the hook and I was gutted. The guide looked at me and said bad luck as he knew I had done my job. It had been a good day and my first initiation into the art of tarpon fishing. It was soon time to head back to camp. I walked back with the evening sun on my back, it felt good but I knew the fish had eluded me once again.

Once more I awoke to clear blue skies, it was my last day's fishing. I ached for a tarpon. The morning produced no fish as the flats were quiet. Naturally, I was disappointed. The guide suggested we go for a permit using fresh crab he had in his live well. I explained I was here for tarpon and nothing else. He understood and we sped off in the hope of finding them again. The boat was fast and we sped under one of the huge bridges before searching an area close to some mangroves. The guide spotted tarpon; I cast to them and realised they were babies. One chased the fly but it didn't take. I knew the big fish lay in the ocean, and he was filling in time. When the tide again started to run the engine roared into action and we were off. After my two days' training I was ready. We searched all afternoon for the tarpon but they didn't appear; it was late in the day and we were staking out the famous Bahia Honda, a stunning flat. Nothing had happened. I was watching and twitching, eager for them to show where they were. I stood rod in hand while the guide scanned the flat. "There," he said and pointed straight ahead, far off down the flat. I saw them, black shapes at first then splashing as they broke the surface before they porpoised and breathed air.

They looked to be moving slowly but they were soon on us, a huge school of maybe one hundred fish or more. I waited with my heart in my mouth for them to come into casting distance. I could see the lead fish, a monster well over 150lb; she stood out as the rest of the school had jet black backs whereas hers was brown. She led alone every now and then, using her head to nudge the fish to her flanks to show her authority. I stood with my rod in my hand watching them approach but just as I was about to cast, a black cloud appeared out of nowhere. I couldn't see! I cast in hope again and again but because I was effectively blind and casting at random the school was spooked and scattered. I looked at the guide and he looked at me. "Bad luck," he said. It was my final chance.

The engine was started and it was time to return to the dock. On the way back the guide told me he wasn't booked for the next day. I explained that I needed the rest of what little money I had left as I was flying off to Belize to fish. I paid him in traveller's cheques then we said our goodbyes and he left. On returning to my tent I noticed a Key's deer appear out of the bush. I sat and watched the sunset and thought of those huge tarpon. I'd tasted fly fishing for tarpon and had loved it but as ever, money had been the decisive factor.

I left the next morning for Key West to spend time getting drunk, chasing women and listening to music before leaving for Miami and heading for Belize. Key West smelt of bygone years. I left on the Greyhound bus three days later hungover.

The flight to Belize didn't take long, three hours or so and clearing customs felt like I'd been slung from one culture to the other, which, lets face it, I had.

David didn't know what I'd been through but you just have to keep some things to yourself. That morning we waded in search of bonefish. Nothing appeared. There had been a hurricane a couple of years before. David, a diver, explained this to me as he had seen the destruction of the coral. I don't think it affected the bonefish, just shook things up a bit. Late in the day we were still wading. I spotted fish - not bonefish but permit! Like rats they moved, their tails and black fins poked out of the shallow water as they approached, searching out crabs in the coral. "There," I said, as I pointed them out to David, who was in front of me. They were coming closer as I shouted, "Cast, cast!" He had spotted them too late and by the time he tried to cast to them they were among our feet and fled - and boy, did they move! They were big permit, hook one of those up and you would know about it I thought to myself! It was an insight into why they were so highly prized by fly fishermen. We waded back to camp with me wishing I was in front of David.

It was obvious after a week of wading the flats the bonefish weren't there. I was to find out David had money as he was an accountant by trade. He had arranged with the divemaster to take us to Turneffe Atoll the next day, famous for its bonefish, about a three hour boat ride. He had come up with the plan the night before and it was where I yearned to go, but I couldn't afford it. So when he gave me the opportunity of joining him I jumped at the chance.

The following morning we packed our gear said our goodbyes and made for the boat. After loading up we sped off across the lagoon. It felt good to leave. I gazed back at the tiny key as we left, watching it until it disappeared on the horizon. When we hit the open marine blue of the ocean the boat slowed and we rigged up two rods and trolled two rapalas. We fished for half an hour or so with no takes; the sea was calm and conditions perfect. We spotted seaweed in the vastness of the ocean and driftwood which was a haven for baitfish; hopefully a predator would be about. We approached slowly as the rapalas searched the depths for fish. Then, quite out of the blue, David's rod slammed over it was bent double. We all watched on in amazement as a marlin took to the air and quickly spat the hook. We looked at each other, stunned, saying nothing, as words weren't needed. That day nothing else happened so we pulled the lines in and powered off to Turneffe.

It was not long until the islands started to appear on the horizon. When they came into view bonefish flats were everywhere. The boat engine slowed and the boat was beached next to a shack on stilts. We clambered off the boat and unloaded our gear. Two rough, stringy Belizians came out to greet us; it was the divemaster's friends, lobster fishermen.

Their shack on the tiny key was the only habitation for miles, built on stilts to protect them from the sea and sandflies and also to light a fire under them in the evenings to keep of the mosquitoes. It was rough. When I say the place was rough I mean rough and coming from me that's saying something as I've roughed it with the best of them. David and I were given the only beds in the shack. I was glad I'd brought an inflatable mattress, as the bed looked like it had never been cleaned. I laughed as David looked at me that evening in the twilight, wishing he had one too.

Lobster fisherman's shack.

The lobster fishermen's hospitality was second to none. That night they made supper, and served two plates of food. I feared the worst but took a mouthful. In fact it proved to be the best meal I'd had and I've never had anything as tasty since. Tiger lobster, freshly pulled from their pots, the rice cooked in fresh coconut milk. It was delicious! I wondered where they had disappeared to in the twilight.

After supper we lay outside in their hammocks made from fishing nets while gazing at the stars. David began to chuckle as he told me how he had watched my eyes grow as big as saucers when I took my first mouthful. He was a cook so he knew just how good they tasted. We talked for a while then went to the smoke-filled hut to get some sleep. The situation felt bizarre, with two Belizian lobster fishermen, an American and me, an Englishman, all crammed into a hut barely big enough to swing a cat in.

Morning came and as ever black coffee kick-started us into gear. I strolled down the shore alone and gazed around. We were surrounded by bonefish flats. Across the deep channel separating us from a nearby key, bonefish tails glistened in the early morning sun. Naturally, I wanted to swim across there and then. I raced back to the shack to find David and the lobster fisherman; we quickly grabbed our rods, hopped into the boat and got dropped off to wade the flats. The lobster fishermen left to check their pots and arranged to meet us later.

Neither of us had seen the like before: so many

bonefish tailing everywhere; it looked too good to be true. However, although we chased and cast to them all morning, they acted like trout in a stew pond. Something was wrong. I could only think they must have been hammered by fly fishermen. Belize is on the doorstep of the States and after encountering the same situation four days on the trot it just confirmed my belief. We caught just one fish between us, although it was a real beauty of 6lb, which fell to my rod. The evenings were made easier by fresh lobster and coconut rice. I explained to David this wasn't normal behaviour for bonefish and told him of the bonefish of Venezuela. It was the first time he had fished for them so he'd been lucky bumping into me as otherwise he would have thought this was the norm. We both left on the fifth day scratching our heads, bonefish were everywhere but the major problem was that they were spooked bonefish. The lobster fishermen took us back into Belize City; it felt good to return after the disappointment of Turneffe. Crossing the Channel, David propositioned me. I'd talked of my tarpon mission in the evenings; he was intrigued, and I think he respected my determination. "Why not let me help you fulfil your dream?" he said.

"How?" I replied.

"Why don't we hire a guide?"

"Because I'm poor and can't afford it," was my answer."

"That's okay, come as my guest." I was too proud to accept at first but during the two hour or so boat trip back to the mainland he persuaded me.

The lobster fishermen knew of a place where we could stay, a defunct fishing lodge a forty-minute or so boat ride up the Belizian River. After a brief stop to have a beer at a local marine side cafe and to pick up the lobster fishermen's women, we left the city to find the lodge.

We followed the coast for a while until we found the entrance to the river. The scenery changed as we left the open sea and once more headed up the river. The jungle was thick on both banks and the river was calm. Along the way we spotted a large caiman basking on a log. As we passed, it slid off into the water for cover and sounds of howler monkeys could be heard, their calls being echoed in the jungle's tree tops. We turned a corner and there it was! The defunct fishing lodge on a bend in the river. It was aptly named Riverbend Resort. We pulled into a small wooden jetty and tied up. From the main house a girl walked down to greet us; she was a Canadian named Laura and, 'a real piece of work'. I instantly liked her. She showed us to one of the three cabins in the grounds, which was built on stilts and situated right on the river front. It was clean but simple and felt like a palace compared to the lobster fishermen's place. A veranda contained two hammocks to watch the wildlife and it was a perfect base for two fishermen.

We unloaded our gear and said our goodbyes to the fishermen. I watched them leave until the boat disappeared around the river bend and the sound of the outboard was gone. We then settled in, it was late afternoon. That night at dinner Laura told us of a guide. "Richard, he's the best!" I was sceptical but Laura rang him to arrange a meeting. She returned from the kitchen and told us he would come to the lodge the following evening. We agreed then headed back to our cabin to sleep.

The next day we played cards as we were waiting. David was drinking tonic water, me a can of beer. He told me why. "I used to enjoy alcohol too much!" was all he said. I understood. That night after supper we were still waiting for the guide. He finally arrived and to be honest I wasn't impressed he was late. I was sceptical but David booked him for the next three days' tarpon fishing.

Early the next day we crossed the Belizian River

by dinghy before being taken by a four-wheel drive to find the local marina and Richard. Shortly afterwards we climbed aboard and left. It was a short ride down the river and again we entered the open sea. Richard was a larger-than-life character, always a smile on his face and very laid back. First he took us to catch live bait as I'd told him the night before about my mission for a giant tarpon. "Live bait," was all he said and we agreed that fly fishing could wait!

After catching the live bait we left to find the tarpon. The engine was stopped and we cast out the live baits swimming under floats. We watched them intently, prepared for a strike, drifting a deep channel. Every now and them a tarpon would roll and breathe air, the Caribbean sun lighting up its back. Blink and you'd miss it. It felt exciting. An hour or so passed and my float disappeared. I struck and was into my first tarpon. It instantly leaped revealing itself as a small fish of around 70lb. After twenty minutes or so I was waist deep in water holding my first tarpon and its beauty was staggering. After trophy shots I released it to fight another day.

We carried on fishing but to no avail. It was time to leave, to fish another deep channel. The anchor was pulled and we sped off across the flats.

Holding my first tarpon.

After twenty minutes or so we again stopped and once more hooked on live baits and cast them out again, watching the floats for a take. It came again, my float disappeared, I struck and was hooked up to a monster tarpon. The first run was blistering as I tightened up on the fish. As it ran it leapt... "Christ, it's huge!" I shouted, David and the guide stayed quiet. They knew I'd hooked a huge fish. The rod was bent double as the engine started and we began to follow it. It was massive and I just prayed the hook would hold. Which much to my relief it did!

Belize, Central America.

I think this extract from my diary best describe the day's events:

Monday 14th June 1999.

I've bloody done it! What an incredible day. Started early at 5.30am, out fishing by 6.30am. Caught live bait, ready to fish. Richard took us to a deep channel and we saw a lot of tarpon rolling, a beautiful sight. No takes so we moved to catch more bait. Whilst fishing we saw a manatee swim right under the boat. After catching live bait we again moved to Long Key and I hooked and landed my first tarpon, estimated at between 65lb and 70lb. Think I got some good shots holding it in the water, let's hope they develop okay. It really was amazing to finally get to see up close one of these amazing creatures. The feeling I got holding one of those fish in the water is indescribable and will stay with me all my life. After it recovered, it swam away full of power back to where it belongs. We moved back to where we had seen the tarpon rolling earlier and at around 12.15pm one took my live bait. I hit it and it immediately leapt into the air, it was

130lb tarpon, mission accomplished!

enormous. It tore line off the reel with incredible power, leaping then bored deep. This fish was really strong and the muscles in my upper body burned under the strain. The fight from the fish was amazing! Every time I thought it would tire it just ran and ran, not giving an inch. After what turned out to be an hour and a half fight, at around 1.45pm it finally succumbed and Richard and I heaved it aboard. It took the two of us to lift it up for the trophy shot. We estimated it to weigh 130lb; it was at least seven feet long. It was the tarpon I had been struggling all this time to catch, making all the pain, frustration, work and sometimes judging my sanity all worthwhile.

That night back at the River Bend Resort I had a beer or two in the hammocks while talking with David. I felt elated. He smiled, as he knew he had helped me fulfil a dream. We got to know each other in those few evenings as we lay in the porch hammocks and talked! He told stories of his father, a rum-runner who flew B52's years before. Now I knew where the glint in his eye had came from. After

Gaffed tarpon.

dinner we both slept well, with me hoping it would be David's turn in the morning. When morning came we met Richard who was on time. The engine was started and we left, speeding down the Belizian River. Howler monkeys screamed from the jungle tree tops as we left the river and entered the open sea off to find the tarpon.

Tuesday 15th June 1999.

Got up early at 4.30am feeling really tired, aching all over from the previous day.. Weather was really bad, reached the marina at 6.30am. The rain and wind would have made fishing impossible so we returned to Riverbend Resort to wait for the weather to hopefully change. Luckily it did and we were soon speeding out to fish. We quickly got some live bait and rigged up. David was to have all the rods to give him a good chance at a tarpon. The first rod was put out straight away and was hit by a fish. David struck it and the fish tore off and leapt - a tarpon! It all happened so quickly and I prayed it would stay on. It was around 10.30am at the time and at around 11.15am David had landed his first tarpon of *around 70lb. Brilliant! It meant we both had caught one now. After taking pictures we released it and it swam away, leaving David with a big grin on his face. Weather continued getting better and even saw dolphin. A brilliant day.*

David & his first tarpon.

When morning came we left the lodge, each of us with a tarpon under our belts. We knew we could relax and enjoy our final day's fishing with the pressure taken off. Again, the day started with us catching live bait then we returned to the channel, where I'd caught the huge fish two days previously. The sun was up and was stifling. We all watched on as the floats bobbed in the sea, it was not until late afternoon that my float again disappeared. I struck. As soon as the tarpon leapt I knew it was huge, the ferocity of the leaping was quite unbelievable and again the engine was started and we followed the fish. "Sorry, David" was all I could say as we chased the fish. He smiled, Like me, he knew that where fishing was concerned expect the unexpected.

Wednesday 16th June 1999.

Got up again at 4.30am and was speeding out by 6.00am. We were met by a large school of Jack Cravelle. We both grabbed fly rods and each hooked a fish at the same time! They were around 10lb and fought like hell, a brilliant and unexpected way to start the day. We then quickly got some live bait, watching the dolphins as we fished and were soon at Map Key where we had been catching the tarpon. At around 10.15am I hooked a fish. It really tore off and took nearly all the line from the reel making an incredible leap in a bid for freedom. It looked huge! It fought really hard making incredible runs. At around 11.00am I had the tarpon in my arms, a huge fish and second estimated at well over a 100lb. I couldn't believe it! The fish looked really tired and I started to get worried. Again and again I tried reviving it and after an hour I knew it was close to death. I felt terrible and sick to the core! Finally we gave up and hauled the huge fish onto the boat. We took it to a nearby fisherman and his wife who gladly took it. At

My smile hides my despair.

A 100lb tarpon in my arms.

least it wouldn't go to waste, but still left me feeling empty. It's times like this I really have to ask myself why I do what I do. I'm a fisherman, no more, no less, and from time to time I realise this will happen. But this still makes it no easier to hold such a majestic creature in your arms, watching its life fade. But I know I will always fish.

At the end of the fishing David again propositioned me. "I don't want to interrupt your trip," he said, "but why don't we go and chase those bonefish in Venezuela? I can meet you in Houston, obviously I will pay for your flight down to Caracas." It was an offer I just couldn't refuse! I explained to him before leaving Central America I had one last thing I must do before joining him, to travel by local bus to Guatemala to see the famous Mayan site of Tikal. The next day we said our goodbyes, I thanked him for the tarpon fishing and arranged to meet a week or so later in Houston before going our separate ways.

Hooked tarpon.

Chapter 3.

Florida Keys,
Christmas Island, Belize.

$\mathcal{N}$ eedless to say when I met David in Houston we made it to Los Roques, Venezuela, we had an amazing time, it was perfection.

Perfection.

During those two weeks David propositioned me again. "I have a year to spare, why not become my guide?" At first I refused but after returning to England I e-mailed him and accepted. He was canny and said to me once he likes to put an idea into someone's head and then let it settle. It certainly worked with me!

Flying out to meet David felt weird. Apart from £400 in my pocket as a backup plan if things went wrong I was in his hands. It felt great to be once again leaving behind the UK and all its pressures, but usually I am my own man and knew that this time, perhaps more than ever, it was going to be tough, relying on someone else was going against the current. The aeroplane finally took off from London Heathrow as it had been delayed. I was brought peanuts then a stiff drink, a bacardi and coke, I needed it as knew I was taking on a lot.

David met me in Miami. He looked stressed, perhaps because the flight had been delayed, but from that moment he somehow looked different from usual, not light-hearted but businesslike - a bad sign. As ever, I shrugged it off and shook his hand; it was good to see him again and after all, he had done most of the planning. The next ten days or so we spent travelling all over Florida in search of a flats boat. We ended up in Key West on the very tip of Florida Keys where we found the boat. It was perfect and definitely the tool for the job. It had obviously been used but definitely not abused. A 17ft Action Craft, it was the boat we were after. Only a few days earlier David and I had visited the factory where they were built. I drove it across the flats of Key

West, the wind in my hair, I felt free. We returned to the dock, David shook hands with the owner, made the deal and bought it. That night we went to Schooners Wharf, a famous bar situated right on the ocean front, to celebrate. It was early evening and as the sun started to disappear over the horizon I drank a beer and listened to a local band and watched baby tarpon rolling between the boats. I was excited but David remained businesslike. I shrugged it off and we returned to our cheap hotel to sleep.

Morning came and we left to find the owner and pay him. When David handed him the cheque the boat was ours. We returned to the dock and boatyard where the boat was stored. The rest of the day we spent planning to get it transported to Fort Lauderdale, where a 130hp Honda four-stoke engine was to be fitted before being shrink-wrapped loaded on a cargo ship and put on the slow boat to Belize. Only in America I thought! Once again, the idea was to return there to hunt the tarpon using the defunct fishing lodge Riverbend Resort as our base. David had been in contact with the owner and had arranged everything. It was going to take a while for the boat to get there, about a month or so, and when all the arrangements were done we were to fly to Christmas Island in the South Pacific to chase bonefish and camp out on the flats. I was so excited by the prospect of it all I could hardly control myself! We left Miami on the first leg of our journey then flew to Honolulu, Hawaii. I'd been suffering with my ears and the doctor had put it down to the air-conditioning. I had an infection and it was horribly painful so he gave me a bottle of large pink pills. I knew it was a mistake to take them. It was 10th October, my granfather's birthday, so I had to drink a rum or two to remember him by. What I failed to do was read the bottle's label which in small letters said 'Not to be taken with alcohol'! The next morning, feeling like death warmed up, David explained how I, in my drugged up state, while in the lift to our room, had bumped into a poor tall guy and said, "Christ, who put you in a bucket of shit?" David managed to get me to the room, where I rolled around the bed moaning that I was dying. Luckily, after an hour I came round and passed out.

The next morning we were flying early. David knew I was 'crook' so he upgraded us to first class. I could have kissed him. I pulled the blanket over my head and slept like a log. When we landed in Hawaii the events of the previous night just seemed like a bad dream. Outside the airport we took a taxi, a stretch limousine; it all felt bizarre. The next morning we again left for the airport on the final leg of our journey, a five hour plane ride on Aloha Airlines for our final destination Christmas Island Kiribati in the South Pacific. On landing on the tiny runway on Christmas Island we went through the usual annoying customs procedure. They were surprised as we had brought a boat with us, a Zodiac dinghy complete with Honda 5hp outboard motor. Obviously, it was deflated. David and I had spent a day back in the States looking for a huge holdall in which to put it, which we eventually found in a local market. We left the shack of an airport and were taken by car to the capital, London. We arrived to find the place looking rough. We unloaded our gear and settled into our accommodation after which I sat and watched the locals. A truck pulled up full of them; they were obviously drunk. A local guide staggered in and showed us his flies. They were the same as mine. We still hired him to take us our supplies and the zodiac out to the flats, to where we were to make camp! I had a bad feeling about the place and the wind was howling which made me feel even more uncomfortable. That night both of us both slept well. When I awoke, the first thing I heard was the wind. After much needed black coffee David and I inflated the Zodiac. Then we headed off to find petrol which we duly purchased from the only dive operation on the island ran by an American. The first thing I noticed was his red derelict Honda XR250 motorcycle. I had a Honda XR500 back home so I wanted the front light and clocks as they were hard to come by. After buying the petrol we returned to the Zodiac. I syphoned the petrol from the plastic fuel tank but sucked too hard and after spitting out a whole mouthful of petrol and connecting the pipe to the outboard my mouth burned. I could still taste it an hour later. The rest of the day was spent buying supplies, enough to last us for the next two weeks in camp as we were to head out in the morning. That evening I sat drinking a beer. David still wasn't feeling himself as he was in business mode, worried about the boat. I tried to be lighthearted and when I turned in for the night I lay there hoping the wind would drop. Needless to say, when morning came the wind still hadn't died down and when the guide turned up I asked him about it. "Oh," he remarked, "it's always like this". I knew from that moment we were in trouble. I said nothing. After loading supplies on the guide's wooden boat we strapped the Zodiac to the front. With the wind still raging I knew we would never use it. As we headed out the wind was still raging and we were in the shelter of the lagoon, not the open sea. After an hour or so we spotted land and David and I looked for suitable camping spots. We were in the teeth of the wind. David suggested a spot and we carried on. Even the boobies looked windswept, huddled together on the shore, occasionally one would fly and land on the boat and stare on at the proceedings.

Finally we found a place - a huge moonscape and a bonefish flat stretching for miles. David wanted to camp on it in the wind. "No," I said. It was a good flat, the saving grace was that I could see palm trees and bush on the shore, a long way off but it had to do, so we set off in the Zodiac and we carted our gear into camp. It was a hell of a job as it was half an hour walk from the shore. We left the Zodiac anchored in the tide. After lugging gear into camp, David stood and watched as I cleared the bush with my bare hands. They got cut to hell. Someone had to do it and obviously why he had brought me. We set up camp and afterwards I drank a few beers, thanks to David. He knew I needed it and had a large cooler full of them along with his tonic water. After a good meal the two of us slept like the dead, oblivious to the sound of the wind. When morning came it had, thankfully, dropped considerably and after a cup of black coffee we both made ready to fish. As we left

Bonefishing camp, Christmas Island.

Bonefishing the flats, Christmas Island.

camp David remarked that he felt like a spaceman about to do a moon walk; that summed it up perfectly. A fifteen minute walk followed as the tide came in. I looked at the white elephant of the Zodiac as we went our separate ways to fish. After all the stories and hype I expected Christmas Island to be extra special and that's why David and I were here even though we could have gone pretty well anywhere. All we found after two weeks were small bonefish and constant wind. As expected, the Zodiac was never used as it was just too windy and unsafe. One day I saw locals chasing bonefish into nets to make the local dish, bonefish balls. It answered a lot of questions. David and I left after catching bonefish no bigger than three and a half pounds. It was a sure sign the larger breeding fish were few and far between and had been taken. The boat picked us up six hours late on our final day; they had obviously got drunk, we could smell it on their breath. Still, we managed to make the local radio station for our exploits. We both left for Belize and the boat after swapping the remaining food and water for my Honda XR bits. We were relieved, as it had been a tough time. Twenty hours of travelling was to follow and when David and I led in hammocks in Riverbend Resort we felt as though we had been through a war zone. For an Englishman, this is when humour is really needed but David still was businesslike about everything concerning the boat.

Thursday November 18th 1999.

It's 7.45am and I'm knackered again. Started at 5.30am. Managed to fish until 4.00pm. It really was a beautiful day, not a cloud in the sky. The flats looked incredible and crystal clear. Poled the boat for the first time. Stood on the poling platform really gives you a new perspective. Caught all kinds of fish; snapper, mackerel, and triggerfish to name just a few. This kept us amused while we waited for the big rods with the live snapper to work. Finally had a live bait taken by a tarpon but David didn't get to it quickly enough. Dolphins kept us company all day, one with its baby. They came right up to the boat. To finish off the day we saw a caiman on its log on the river. He's usually there most days, sunbathing, and at around seven feet long is quite a sight.

What happened in Belize I just don't know; the

boat arrived on the slow boat from Fort Lauderdale shrink-wrapped as promised. We put the boat in the water and had it tied up outside Riverbend Resort on its wooden jetty. We had all the tools for the job and were setup with David's money and my experience but somehow it just didn't work, me too free, David holding the cards.

There was one incident however and I shall take the memory of it to my grave. I was driving the boat up the Belizian river, howler monkeys were screaming and a caiman escaped from its usual log as we left the river and entered the open sea. The wind was again in my hair and I felt cut free from the normality of the West. We caught just one fish, a tarpon of 60lb, before returning to camp and as the boat - with its 130hp Honda - hit the quietness of the Belizean river it began to hiss. I opened out the engine adjusted the trim tabs and sped back to camp and the waiting ice cold beer. As I swung from bend to bend I felt I had just had a glimpse of how the rich live.

My fingers went septic after cutting them to pieces on Christmas Island owing to catching reef fish daily for live bait and became infected as the fish carried bugs. I put on a brave face, soaking them in saltwater every night, but I was feeling low. One evening after fishing I decided to leave Belize to continue to follow my dreams. I got drunk and stayed in a cheap hotel only to return the next day to get my rods. Even though things had gone horribly wrong I shook David's hand to thank him for the opportunity and fled back to England to freedom and poverty. On the flight home I felt faint and asked for help from one of the air hostesses. I had to be taken to the toilet as I was feeling dizzy and nearly passed out. On returning to England I went to the Doctor, he told me I had the first stages of septicaemia. Luckily a course of antibiotics sorted it out! I felt I hadn't failed at the last hurdle as I had given it my all!

The boat on the Belizian flats.

Chapter 4.

Somerset, England.

*W*hen I returned from Belize my spirits were at a low ebb. I went to see my brother Peter and we talked for a while. "You know that Airstream trailer you wanted, it's parked up in the turnip field down the road, derelict, you ought to find out about it." I couldn't believe it had turned up again it was a glimmer of hope in the darkness. It felt like it was meant to be and somehow it had been waiting for me to turn up. It looked rough - like me - and out of place in a Somerset turnip field. I badly wanted it but as ever there was one major problem; I was broke. A bungalow lay in sight, obviously belonging to the landowners.

I plucked up courage, tapped on the door and asked about the Airstream. They told me the owner had recently broken down near the road and asked if he could leave it there for a while. "What's his telephone number?" I asked. They gave it to me, somehow I got the feeling he didn't really know what to do with it. I returned home and slept on my mother's couch. The next day, with baited breath, I rang him and told him I was interested in it. Luckily for me, he said he wanted to sell it, I arranged to meet him the next day at the Airstream. That night I

---

was restless and didn't sleep too well. The next morning I rode up on my Honda XR500 motorcycle, eager to meet him, and I had a good look at it. It had been abused, made into a cafe, and it needed help. As a kid I'd caught glimpse's of these amazing caravan's, to me they were impressive pieces of art and I'd always wanted one - this was my chance. A car turned up, and the owner asked me to take a look inside. Rain had got in and it was full of cafe equipment, none of which worked, and stainless steel covered the inside, smothering the windows and skylights. However, despite the mess I could see its potential. "How much do you want?" I asked.

"Five thousand pounds," he replied. It was probably worth that even in its current state.

Nevertheless, I haggled until finally I said, "I'll give you three thousand pounds, it's all I have." I expected him to refuse, but he didn't. It was mine!

"Pay me half the money and it's yours", he said, "I can wait a while for the other half." We shook on it. I left, desperate to raise the cash. Half I borrowed from Peter the rest I borrowed from my grandmother. I rang the owner of the Airstream a few days later and arranged to meet him there. When he turned up I gave him the deposit and he handed me the keys, now it really was mine. I couldn't believe it! The first thing I had to do was to move it. Peter borrowed his boss's four-wheel drive and we towed it away and parked it outside his workshop. I needed work, I took a job there as a dogsbody again. I'd been here before but with the Airstream parked outside it was a constant reminder why! Just being in the Airstream felt exciting, it was a truly incredible space.

Inside the Airstream before work started, a blank canvas.

All my spare time was spent working on the Airstream; like everything I'm passionate about, I was obsessive about it! It was a huge task. The worst problem was the floor, water had got in and it was rotted. Having been converted to a cafe the inside was covered in diamond-patterned stainless steel covering everything in its path including the skylights and windows. I knew if left it would make the space amazing, but I knew it would be a nightmare of a job. After emptying the interior of all the broken down cafe gear I was finally left with a blank canvas with which to work. As the weeks, which quickly turned into months, went by I began to turn a corner and the Airstream began to take shape. I'd cut the ends off my fingers daily on the stainless steel, and it was terribly painful. Eventually the light began once again to pour in from the windows and skylights. I left the UK once more to chase fish. After I had replaced the entire floor and insulated its double skin it was put into storage until I returned. I flew to Canada to chase Steelhead on the famous Skeena river. It was flooded, so I fled to Miami to get drunk before continuing to Venezuela to chase bonefish. I wasn't disappointed and the fishing was amazing. When I returned to the UK I had just enough money left to tow the Airstream to Cornwall. My mother had bought an old derelict chapel there. I turned up broke but for once, at least I had some kind of home. I was thirty three at the time. I slept on the floor on a mattress with only candles for light but somehow it felt right.

The Airstream in Cornwall.

I went to Venezuela bonefishing twice during a period of a couple of years. I worked daily finishing the Airstream. In truth, I begged, borrowed and stole everything that was needed to complete it. Finally, in 2002, I towed it back to Somerset, again put it in storage then left to fish, first to Cairns to learn to dive, then onto Tasmania, finally arriving in New Zealand to chase trout. Two months later I returned happy in the knowledge I had again nailed a few.

The excitement waned and with the Airstream in storage, no job and nowhere to live, I was in some sorry state. I slept on my mother's couch. One night I found my grandfather's half bottle of rum and drank the whole contents. The next day, with fire in my belly, I found a job and a place to put the Airstream, providing me with somewhere to live. My grandfather was looking after me!

The Airstream in Somerset.

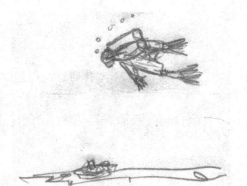

Chapter 5.

Bay of Islands, Honduros.

*T*he very name Mosquito Coast makes me dream of travel. I knew I had to go someday, which is what happened in 2002. I'd just returned from Tasmania, Australia, and Taupo in New Zealand, trout fishing. I felt as though I was in transit as I'd spent no more than a couple of days back in the UK. I made the fatal mistake of going to the pub, getting blind drunk then somehow staggering home. My brother Peter drank with me that night. He knew I had drunk too much but we headed home in different directions. What I failed to tell him was that I was scared. I awoke the next morning feeling like death warmed up. I was driven the one hundred and eighty miles to Cornwall and once again bumped into my uncles (on my mother's and grandmother's side). The car was stopped in Glastonbury and as my mother and grandmother looked at a sculpture I spewed up. Half way to Cornwall I rang my other uncle, Julian, back in Somerset. He laughed and said, "True to form!" It was he who thirty years earlier took me fishing to the local trout stream after I'd lain on the bed and cried for hours because he had taken my older brother James instead of me. He took me the next day and I caught my very first wild brown trout!

We arrived just before dark. One uncle lived in a house, the other in an old church brought down in the sixties on a lorry. Peter lived in the church and is a musician; Bernard, my other uncle, lived in the house and like Julian had taught me to fish, constantly feeding me fishing books (he still does to this day despite being into his seventies).

I knew Honduros was very dangerous but I didn't care, I just had to go. That evening I sat outside in the cold with Peter, wrapped in blankets drinking cider, a night I will never forget and just what I needed. He played his guitar for hours. The next evening I left by coach from Truro in Cornwall bound for Heathrow Airport, London. Bernard waved goodbye as my mother looked on, standing in the rain. She knew it was once again time for me to leave.

While I was on the coach I managed to sleep, though only spasmodically as I knew it was going to be dangerous. I was once again going to have to live off my wits. Again I drifted in and out of sleep in the warmth and security of the coach. On arriving at Heathrow Airport I checked in, then went to the bar.

I landed in Houston in the US, a hub for Central America. After waiting in transit for an hour or so again I boarded the plane and found a seat. The flight took off and I asked for a bacardi, as I needed a stiff drink. The peanuts and the bacardi were brought and I sat back thinking how exciting it all was. I was ready to fish and thankfully in my old age I had not calmed down.

After arriving in the capital Tegucigalpa I left the airport. I crossed the bridge toward the local bank to change some money. Outside, security consisted of a guy with a sawn-off, loaded shotgun and he nodded as I entered. As I was waiting in the queue, he entered. Everyone looked at me, it was just a twenty minute walk from the relative safety of the airport and it made me realise this was a very dangerous country. I left after changing my dollars into the local currency (lempira), followed again by the guy with the shotgun until I left the bank. He watched on as I crossed back over the bridge. Again I entered the airport, glad to be flying, first for Le Ceba and the airport on the coast before flying onto the Bay of Islands. With a wad of money in my wallet, I was full of intrepidation waiting for the plane. By the time it was time to leave I was relieved to get going again. The flight was a short one; after about an hour we landed and after a delay of a further hour I boarded the plane to fly me to Utilia. On landing in Utilia I was taken to the main township, a ramshackle place, a backpacker's outback for diving. After doing some research, I knew it held some of the cheapest and best diving in the world. I had given myself a birthday present three months earlier in Cairns, Australia, of an open water PADA diver's course on the Great Barrier Reef, it was my back up plan. Being a fisherman, I was seeking fresh territory for bonefish but after asking around it was quite obvious they lay elsewhere. Although I did find them on a flat near the airport they were sparce and the scenery was so ugly I decided to dive. I booked five days diving; ten dives in which to see the wildlife. What followed blew my mind: the coral, the reefs and its fish. The crystal clear water offered stunning visibility of over forty metres gin-clear and as warm as toast. I'd hopefully come to see a whale shark, the biggest fish in the ocean, but being a fisherman I'd managed to see something better. On one dive I glanced to the surface and watched on in wonder as a whole patrol of tarpon passed by. They were huge. They were gone as quickly as they had appeared and left me thinking it had been an amazing dream. The rest of the divers hadn't seen them. After the diving, I left, again hoping I'd find bonefish over on the next island in the chain Guanaja. It looked to be a very strange place, I thought as the plane landed on the runway. Speed boats were waiting to take folk to the main town. It was situated about a fifteen minute boat ride off the shore on a tiny key in which to escape the sandflies, as on the mainland they were veracious. After being dropped off with my gear on the wooden wharf, the first thing I noticed was a ten foot square concrete building with no windows, the prison. The tiny key was so tiny you could walk around it in well under an hour. It had no beaches, just a shanty town smothered in wooden shacks. That night I went into one of the local hangouts and drank beer. I was the only Westerner on the island. I found out a woman had been raped the night before and the perpetrator was being held in the tiny concrete box, waiting to be taken to the mainland the following day in order to be hung. The bar was dangerous. One guy tried to rob me but unsuccessfully as I'd paid a local to look after me. It felt really dangerous and after having found a cheap room I had difficulty in getting some sleep. The next day I bought a huge shell from a local vendor who was selling such items in one of the maze of dusty streets. He cut the end off and blew into it causing it to give out a haunting sound. I bought it cheaply as knew my brother Paul, being a sculptor, would love it.

Giant shell, Guanaja.

The next day after asking around I met a local fisherman with a boat and arranged to stay with him and his family. He also agreed to take me around the island in search of bonefish. After all, that was what I had come here for. His place was on the main island, on the shore, but somehow it escaped the sandflies. Over the next two days he took me all over the island, dropping me off on the shore whenever it was possible. I managed to catch some bonefish but they were average size and few and far between. I stood on the front of his wooden boat, scanning the

94

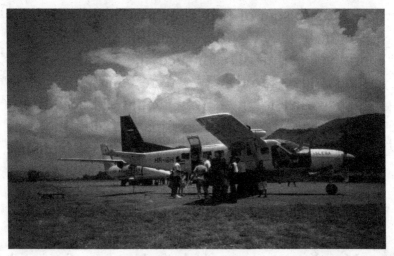

Guanaja's tiny airport.

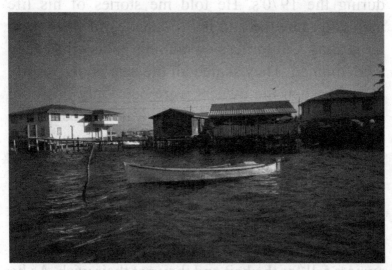

Fishermans boat, Guanaja.

flats for any sign of fish. I saw nothing for an hour or so then they appeared out of the blue, three enormous permit. I estimated the smallest to be around 30lb, the other two were even bigger. The fishing wasn't for me. Even though I'd seen those huge fish, the bonefish were sparce. I left the next morning on the local fisherman's boat. He wouldn't fish that day anyway as it was a Sabbath so, trying to maximise my money, he dropped me off at the tiny airport so leaving him time to pray and me to get the flight to Roatan so as to dive.

My dive partner used to be a professional skateboarder, a hangover from the pursuit's heyday during the 1970's. He told me stories of his life including, how he and his friends learnt their trade by skating California's swimming pools when they were drained. They skated all the best pools, mostly at night when the owners were out. Only one pool eluded them and of course it was the best. The owners were always there so they came up with a plan. One of the skateboarder's was a builder so they decided to crash an old car into the surrounding wall in the dead of night. He returned the next day and innocently offered to fix the wall for free as long as he and his mates were allowed to skate the pool. The owners fell for the bait and they got their wish. As he told me the story I imagined him as a youngster. I looked at him and could see life had taken its toll.

Sunday 12th May 2002.

It was boiling hot last night, had to take a shower in the night to cool off. The diving was incredible, three dives the longest lasting over an hour. The sea was crystal clear and the fish and coral amazing. Saw a turtle on the first dive. The day started well, hummingbirds flying through and around the cafe whilst I ate breakfast. They are so tiny. This was followed by a dive, a wonderful way to start any day. The last dive was spectacular, swimming through underwater caves sprinkled with shoals of fish, the light beaming through. Tomorrow, another two more dives, the first is on a wreck 110 feet down.

Over the next week we shared more than ten dives, each one was special. The best was on a wreck and as we dived I felt like a freefalling skydiver. Visibility was forty metres and as we dropped to the wreck in a crystal clear column of water, huge groupers came to greet us, even a large moray eel came out to say hello, it was truly amazing.

I also experienced night diving. One evening we all headed out and entered the water as the light began to fade; when night fell we all switched off our torches and sat in a circle on the ocean floor. We wiggled our hands and fingers and the plankton lit up luminous in the darkness like stardust and went to the surface in a circle. I was cave diving one day and gazed at the light coming though the holes in the coral. It felt like being in a cathedral and as we passed through the chambers a hidden school of baitfish schooled in the darkness, their scales glistening from the light coming through a hole in the cave as they circled for safety. I left Honduros with a hangover as on the last night I played pool against the locals and drank into the early hours. I returned to England after completing over twenty dives to once again catch my breath. As usual it had been a crazy time!

Chapter 6.

Guayana, Venezuela.

It was in 1998 whilst travelling around Venezuela I first learnt of an amazing fish. I'd been out on the islands camped on the beach for the last month, bonefishing, so I looked pretty rough. On returning to the mainland I scrubbed myself up and managed to blag my way into the marlin fishing club to drink beer and look at the photographs. I was handed a brochure with the usual stuff on marlin fishing but the photograph on the centre page made my jaw drop! What the hell was this fish? Big and silver but with one distinct feature - huge fangs! The caption read payara.

Venezuelan payara.

I found out they live in the fast flowing turbulent rivers of the interior of the country. I decided at that moment to travel by local bus to try and search them out. After a week or so I found myself in a rough gold mining town on the Paragua River. No one spoke any English except a black guy who had lived with the missionaries in French Guayana. I plied him with the local beer (polar) to try to loosen his tongue; he then switched to drinking rum and got crazier by the minute. He was carrying a knife; first he started on his friends then by the end of the night he started on me. I can look after myself, but he looked tough, stringy and muscly with a huge scar across his torso. I tried blagging my way out of the situation but he followed me all the way back to my room, threatening me with the knife and asking for money, his other hand clutching a bottle of rum. I slammed the door in his face and bolted the lock. The door was made of steel, I quickly realised why. The room was rough, dark and sweaty with a dirty mattress, no windows, a muddy bucket of river water in which to wash and a single light bulb, it was no more than a prison cell. The next morning I awoke to a knock on the door, room service I thought to myself, I was wrong it was the crazy guy still with the knife in one hand and half a bottle of rum in the other, it was as though he hadn't left. Things got very dangerous and I fled back to the coast.

I was determined to return one day which five years later I did! The picture in the marlin club had been etched on my brain; I was scared to go back but it seemed as though every time I got drunk I felt I had to return. I bit the bullet and joined an agency in the UK, eight months of doing the most horrible factory jobs were to follow. I ended up at a babyfood factory. Out of all the tempory jobs it was the easiest, but I still hated every minute of it even though I knew it was a one off, so desperate to return to Venezuela, I stuck at it. What kept me going was the fact I promised myself daily I would never do it again! Before I was due to leave, Venezuela was in chaos. There was a strike, people were being shot daily in the streets, the British Foreign Office warned people not to travel. The opportunity was limited and I was frantic. A week before I was due to leave, the Foreign Office said it was now safe to travel so the company rang me from the States, the trip was back on. They warned me there was still some danger but I didn't care. I wasn't going to fail at the last hurdle. I flew to Caracas, relieved just to be going there but I still felt uncomfortable. I felt something would go wrong and it did. On landing in

Guayana, Venezuela.

Caracas I found, to my horror, my bag containing all my fishing gear had been left in Amsterdam Airport. I had my rods but nothing else. I waited for around twenty four hours, hoping the bag would turn up. It didn't. I had to fly the next day to the interior of the country. My contacts said they would send the bag to me and not to worry but I left Caracas frantic with worry. I was met by my interpreter at the Puerto Ordaz airport. I was not happy at being in a sweaty tropical city without my bag. He drove me to my accommodation and said he would meet me in the morning. A sleepless night followed, no camera, no reels, no lures, the list went on. I awoke and went for coffee; black, I needed it! The interrupter turned up late. He suggested we go on down to the jungle and camp. I told him without the bag I didn't intend to go anywhere. Even beer that day didn't get rid of my worry. Later that evening we returned back to the airport and waited for the flight from Caracas to get in. I was at the end of my tether. I watched in slow motion as the bags came down the rough conveyer belt, it was horrible having to wait. Then I saw it, my bag! I grabbed it and shook the hand of the interpreter. The camp owner turned up in his four-wheel drive then we were off. Thank god!!

On leaving the airport the camp owner explained

via the interpreter why he had been late. That very morning he and his family had been held up at gunpoint. He explained how while he was sitting around eating breakfast, gunmen burst in and stole the family jewellery. He acted as though this was an everyday event. Somehow, I knew he would get it back. I sat in the four-wheel drive and stared out at the passing scenery. I felt numb but I knew the trip for payara was on! A three-hour journey was to follow. On the way down to the jungle, the camp owner asked how many women I wanted. Jokingly, I said two. The interpreter had to explain I was joking, as he wasn't.

I found myself back in the same gold mining town as five years previously but this time with support. Unfortunately my arranged accommodation was closed and by a twist of fate I found myself back in the same rough hotel with steel door and bucket of river water. It hadn't changed much and I slept lightly with bad memories. The fishing camp lay up river near a huge waterfall named Uriama Falls. The camp owner had inherited the site, left over by gold miners, from his father and turned it into a fishing camp. It was where huge trophy payara had been caught. A light aircraft, along with the translator, flew me into the camp about an hour up river. We followed the course of the river until finally a tiny landing strip could be seen cut out in the jungle. Even the pilot looked scared as we approached to land! But after a bumpy landing we grounded safely. On walking into camp I was met by the guide and boatman and after breakfast I headed out to fish. I attached a 22cm rapala to 200yds of 65lb braid on my 7ft spinning rod. The river was breathtaking. We fished water so rapid it was hard to believe anything could live there but soon the huge rapala was snatched and a payara leapt clear of the water, making the ratchet scream, and emptying line from the reel. After a good scrap I was holding my first payara, it must have been around 10lb. What an incredible looking fish, so weird with its huge fangs! These fish have holes in their upper jaw in which to accommodate these teeth. They also have two smaller fangs in their bottom jaw, which are hidden and spring up when they attack. Payara chase their prey to the surface and then twisting their bodies hit prey from the side, a truly ferocious predator. The world record is a fish of 39lb so 10lb is an average size catch. I was here for a big fish of 20lb or more if I could get one, it would be a long awaited dream come true. By the end of the day I'd caught fifteen payara, the highlight a 12lb fish caught at dusk. After

Releasing my first payara.

breakfast and coffee early the next day, we again headed out to fish for payara. I followed the guide and boatman as they led me through the bush and onto the river shore and to the waiting dugout canoe with a beaten-up Yamaha outboard. Neither spoke any English but sometimes, where fishermen are concerned, its not needed as everyone's after the same thing. As we left the shore and found the current, the sun was just starting to rise and the heat was becoming noticeable. Kingfishers perched between the huge boulders, which lined the shore; they were waiting for their early morning feed. The guide selected a lure from my vast collection to attach to my line. After he had clipped it on, I cast it out and we trolled in the beer-coloured, turbulent water. I felt at peace. I could feel the lure quivering in rapids far below in the torrent of water, searching out its first victim, and after half an hour or so it did. The rachet screeched out in protest and the rod jammed hard over as the lure was taken. I was hard fast into a good fish. We all shouted when far down the river we saw a huge payara leaping down the rapids. It instantly spat the hook. We trolled on in anticipation of another strike. Payara because they have so many teeth, you're lucky to land one in every five strikes. It goes with the territory. We returned to

The terror.

Payara I caught at dusk.

camp that day after catching ten payara, all hard fighters, the best a fish of 14lb, but nothing huge. Weary from the heat, I returned back to camp in need of a cold beer. It had been a good day. After supper the cook, the guide, the translator and I played dominoes. Before the generator was turned off I lay in bed writing my diary, I felt lost, a real adventurer. The generator and with it the lights were switched off leaving me to pass out to the sounds of the insects in the jungle. I awoke the next day in the twilight; it was my 36th birthday. Before clambering out of bed I lay for just five minutes and listened to the morning chorus from the birds in the jungle. I felt alive. Walking to the boat that morning after breakfast I decided not to tell the guide or boatman it was my birthday as I didn't want to pressure them.

I was surprised at around 8.30am when the boat was taken to the shore. The guide led me up the rocks and told me to cast into the rapids below. We had been trolling for over an hour with no strikes. I did as I was instructed and began making long casts down the rapids cranking back the huge rapala through the torrent of water. On only the fourth retrieve it was taken with such ferocity it shocked me. The rod bent double and a huge payara leapt and made a huge run down the rapids, again leaping the reel screaming as it went. Even the guide got excited when he saw it as he knew it was a good fish. I just prayed it would stay on. The current was strong and the river, like the payara, was wild. It ran deep into the braid, no longer leaping. I felt it must be well hooked as I hadn't lost it. As it came closer and I fought it in the gin-clear, beer-coloured water I could clearly see it now and as it swam past, it's silver glistening flanks. I was gobsmacked as it was the most amazing creature I had ever seen. Four times it came close; but eventually it tired and the guide who was in the water lifted out my prize, a magnificent trophy payara which we weighed in at twenty five and a half pounds. What a way to celebrate my birthday. Danger! said the guide. As I held it up as he took the trophy shots. Then I revived it and it swam off back into its gothic hell.

Thursday 13th February 2003. 36 today!

To catch a 25lb pound payara on my birthday, which was what happened at around 8.50am, was a dream. I'm here in the Venezuelan jungle holding an incredible fish with huge vampire teeth, what an amazing birthday present. The Paragua River is amazing, so beautiful,

25lb trophy payara.

Payara fangs.

and to be fishing here today is just unbelievable. Hopefully if I can pull it off I will be in India this time next year. Payara though, are the fish of my dreams.

I managed to explain (in my awful Spanish) to the guide and cook that it was my birthday that evening; so after dominoes and me drinking too much beer they understood when I passed out in a hammock. Before switching off the generator they awoke me as they wanted me to sleep well. And I did so content in the knowledge I had landed seven payara including the 25lb fish I had come all his way for.

Payara lower jaw.

The next morning I felt a little worse for wear. I was brought coffee to kick-start me back into gear.

One swig and I had to spit it out as the cook had mistaken the sugar for salt! It was one hell of a wake up call and had to swallow hard but I had to laugh. We all ate payara that morning for breakfast before again heading out into the blistering heat to fish. Over the next two days the fishing got even better and by the end of the week I had landed sixty eight payara, amongst them four fish over 20lb. The camp owner turned up with his lady of the night and while he screwed her in a hammock the rest of us sniggered and played dominoes. He challenged me later to a game of ping pong. It felt bizarre but they had an old table so we decided to play in the middle of the Venezuelan jungle. I felt quietly confident as I played a lot as a boy against my elder brother James. I beat the cook and guide but not him as he was good! Now I knew why he owned the camp! I left camp the next day by light aircraft and after changing aeorplane at Puerto Ordaz, I flew back to Caracas. I ended my trip by once again bonefishing for a couple of weeks before flying home. I caught thirty fish. I left Caracas airport and when drinks were brought I sat back, closed my eyes and reflected upon the fact that this trip more than any had been the best so far.

A trophy payara.

Chapter 7.

Cauvery River, Southern India.

*O*n my 36th birthday I'd set myself a task. I decided while sitting in the payara camp in the Venezuelan jungle that, if I could make it, this time next year I would be in a camp somewhere in India. I knew it was time to get back there to have a chance of catching a giant mahseer, and hopefully to meet Subhan, a river god, and guide on the legendary Cauvery River. There were several camps dotted along the river but I knew that wherever Subhan was meant one thing - mahseer. I knew he was getting on and I felt it would be my one and only chance to fish with this legend. At the time it seemed an impossible dream, but sometimes dreams come true.

After returning from Venezuela I tried tempory work. I'd broken my promise to myself not to go back to the baby food factory; I tried it but it messed me up. I then tried a driving job. Perfect, I thought, I'll be my own man. I was taking painkillers daily and thought it was normal but it wasn't. The pain increased until finally my sciatica returned. On the way to visit my mother I was involved in a minor motorbike accident. I hobbled into the doctor's with a bad back and half-broken ankle. She had no compassion and sent me on my way, I was shocked.

Cauvery River, India.

By a strange twist of fate the accident helped as part of the insurance deal was to see a physio about my ankle. I was sceptical as had seen a few already without success but I thought maybe she would be different as she was private. I met her and realised she was different. The watercolours she had gathered on her walls confirmed this. She gave me reflexology on my feet not for my ankle injury but to help relieve the line of pain down my left leg and back caused by sciatica she realised how much pain I was in and unlike the doctor had compassion. I instantly felt the pain in my leg and back subside just a little but enough to make my life bearable again. It made me believe in the exercise regime she had given me. I topped these up by walking through the woods daily, following a trout stream. Slowly but surely, the pain began to subside in my back and down my leg also my ankle healed. It had taken five months.

The compensation came through. Not much but enough to fish for mahseer again. After countless e-mails and research I found a camp (Bush Betta) situated right on the banks of the Cauvery River in Southern India. I got on the plane at Heathrow and sat on the plane writing my diary. As ever, it had once again been a mad journey to put myself in this position. It felt good though and I knew I would do it again. After my research I knew it was the camp to be in as it was ran by Subhan. I was as excited to meet him as I was to catch mahseer. I'd read about him on and off and his amazing fish, for all of my life, and now I was finally going to meet this river god. With what little money I had, I managed to arrange a month in his camp; it would have been longer if I'd had the money! I just couldn't wait.

I flew from Heathrow to Chennai in India where I changed planes to take a short internal flight to my final destination, Bangalore. On landing, I cleared customs and waited - as ever with great trepidation - for my bag and rods to appear. They finally appeared, much to my relief. I left the sanctuary of the airport and entered into the heat and chaos of India. Outside, amongst the hordes of people, I spotted my contact. He showed me to the waiting car and we left. It was a luxury being met as usually I was alone and had to live off my wits. The drive was to take about three hours. I felt really excited.

It had been seven years since I was last in India trying to catch a big mahseer in Arunachal Pradesh in the far north. After all the fishing and travelling I felt like it had been a different man who had done that. As we headed south and left the city, we passed several villages. After the chaos and squalor of Bangalore it felt good to be in the countryside. After an hour or so we stopped for soft drinks. Various stalls were selling all kinds of goods: flowers were strung like Hawaiian necklaces, hundreds of them hanging there, the colours and scents filling the air with their sweet smells. The women who sold them were dressed in beautifully coloured silk dresses. It was wonderful. As we continued on our journey south the countryside began to get greener and greener. Scooters passed us every now and then with passengers wearing little protection - no helmets, sometimes no shoes. They looked free. I didn't know what to expect when I caught my first glimpse of the river but when I did after all the stories it looked low and my heart sank. We carried on following the river, avoiding the huge granite boulders on the dusty road and finally we stopped. The driver pointed below to a camp; at first I thought it was were the locals lived. I spotted a tree house. He unloaded my gear and I realised it was the fishing camp. I was met by a boy who helped me carry my gear down the hill. On arriving, I was asked where I wanted to stay. "The tree house!" I cried without hesitation.

It was late afternoon when I walked into camp, apart from one guide, it was very quiet. Subhan wasn't there. I felt tired from the flight but as I unpacked, the guide appeared to check my gear. He approved but laughed because as ever I'd brought too much. He disappeared with my rod to set it up. I was to fish just before it got dark. The tree house was quite amazing, very Heath Robinson as they say; with everything lashed together it all worked and it included a toilet and shower.

The tree house.

The gangway to the tree house.

The view over the river from the tree house was breathtaking, in fact it felt like home. I crossed the gangway for the first time then met the guide and we left to fish. There was a huge pool near the camp and it smelt of fish. I didn't expect anything to happen; mahseer are notoriously hard to catch so when after an hour the rod bolted over and I struck I was stunned and I think even the guide was. The first take was quite staggering but I knew when I turned it that it wasn't big and before long a 28lb silver mahseer in all her glory was in my arms. After I had taken photos I left for a beer and an early night, as I was jet lagged. It was a good welcome.

28lb silver mahseer.

I was awoken at three in the morning by the sounds of voices. I gazed across to camp. A group of fishermen were talking and drinking, they had obviously just arrived. I got back into bed and awoke at first light. The sun was rising and I yawned as I got out of bed. As I did so I listened to the roar of the river below. Bleary-eyed, I crossed the gangway to get some breakfast. I was the first up. After meeting the rest of the group, who had turned up in the early hours, we headed off to fish and I met Subhan for the very first time. He was squat on the ground in the dust contentedly overlooking the river he loved so much. If you didn't know who he was or what he had achieved in his life you would have passed him by. Hopefully, one day, I will be like that. It was his camp I was in and like so many great fisherman I've met he was very understated and stayed in the background. He was lovely and we fished together that evening. It was dusk, with me so excited to be fishing with this legend sat next to me I couldn't shut up. He cast the egg-shaped ragi across the river and let it settle behind a rock where mahseer was known to lie. After handing me the rod he told me to be quiet so as not to frighten the fish. We sat together, quietly overlooking the river at sundown. It felt magical and although we returned to camp fishless,

I found the beer tasted sweet that evening.

Subhan and the Cauvery River.

Sitting on a rock all day in a hundred degrees of heat, rod in hand, hour after hour waiting for a bite really takes it out of you both physically and mentally. It felt like a lesson. The river was wild and beautiful and felt mysterious. Monkeys looked on, intrigued by our actions, the heat was sweltering. When evening came, the rocks began to change to a deep red in the evening sun and the heat began to subside. It was a huge relief. The mahseer must have

---

felt the same as they were hiding deep in the cool among the huge boulders. For days I fished on but there was nothing to write home about, just the odd small mahseer. It was frustrating. The first group of eight fishermen left camp with only two big mahseer between them; a 40lb silver mahseer and a 50lb golden mahseer. It was very tough going. With only the 28lb fish under my belt, I knew I was in for a challenge if I was to land a mahseer of any consequence.

I wait for a bite at Camp Pool.

That evening I was alone in the tree house, writing my diary in the lamplight with just the sound of the river below. It was nice to be alone with my thoughts again. By the time the next group had come into camp I was still with no fish and desperately in need of some kind of inspiration.

The first group had caught both the 40lb and 50lb fish from the Camp Pool so I knew it was a good spot. Subhan had been fishing Crocodile Rock. I knew he was there for one reason only - a big mahseer. Everyone wanted to fish with him there of course. Sadly, other guides took me to other pools. Each evening back at camp I always asked the fisherman who had been with Subhan what they had caught. "Only small mahseer," was the usual answer. The new group of fishermen were experienced and well travelled; except for one. When the big mahseer from Crocodile Rock did finally come it fell to his rod. It was dusk. Subhan cast a live fresh crab into the river and before he had a chance to hand over the rod he hooked into a fish. He struck twice as the fish surged upstream to set the hook then he was able to hand over the rod. One of the other guides jumped in, a sure sign of a big mahseer. Like an otter he swam across the river and grabbed the 40lb line before lifting it over his head to free it from the rocks. I clambered up onto the rocks to get a better view and like the monkeys I looked on. From my vantage point I could see the mahseer. It was huge. The battle ensued until the fish finally tired and a golden mahseer of 60lb was on the stringer. I climbed back down and watched in the half light as the trophy shots were taken. It was the fish everyone had been after. The stringer was soon taken out and she was released back to where she belonged. It was the inspiration I needed.

Three days later we fished Jenukal in a huge deep gorge below Mekhedaatu (Goat's Leap). It hadn't been fished for days, it just smelt of fish. The mahseer were there. I could feel it. We were taken by jeep the short drive upriver from camp and clambered down into the gorge to the awaiting coracle where we crossed the river. Four of us fished there that day. Two fishermen were above me perched high upon the rocks whilst Subhan, myself and the last of the group fished on a ledge just below them. We were high up. I cast the ragi into the deep, green, slow and mysterious water far below. Subhan sat next to me in anticipation. Half an hour then passed before the rod bolted over. I struck hard and was into a mahseer and judging by its strength it was a good one. It stayed deep, the rod ached under the pressure and the line tore from the reel as it ripped through the water and up the gorge. The fish began to appear on the surface swimming strongly and I could see its tail patterns. Subhan leapt to his feet and clambered down the rocks waiting for the fish to tire. Much to my relief it did so and he grabbed the mahseer, gently unhooked it and put her on a stringer to recover. I dropped the rod; my hands were shaking and I made my way down to join him. I got into the water waist deep and lifted my prize - a silver mahseer estimated at 45lb by Subhan.

45lb silver mahseer.

The fish was calm now and I released the stringer. I could feel it regain its strength as I held it in the river. Strongly it swam off back into the depths.

After that fish, everything came into place; the river, the wildlife and, of course, the mahseer. I felt in tune with the river.

Another two days passed and the river produced another two good fish for the other fishermen, a 35lb fish and one weighing in at 40lb. One evening I found myself fishing with Subhan again, this time at Crocodile Rock. I cast a live freshwater crab down river, its legs and claws outstretched, acting like air brakes. Ten minutes later the rod was nearly ripped out of my hands as the crab was seized by a very strong mahseer, which tore off downriver. I struggled to hold on. I clambered across the rocks, trying not to slip and managed to stop its first run. Then it turned and headed back upstream. Subhan was next to me and made ready with the stringer. I felt I would surely lose it but as the fight continued it began to tire and soon a bullet shaped 40lb golden mahseer lay at our feet.

Subhan gently unhooked the mahseer and put her on the stringer to recover. Holding that fish in my arms felt special, it was so beautiful and wild. It's golden scales lit up in the evening sun making it look tiger like. After photos had been taken I undid the stringer and released her back into the river where she belonged.

40lb golden mahseer.

I returned back to camp. It was dark by now. That evening I sat drinking beer in good company while the river thundered below. It was what I had imagined mahseer fishing to be like when I'd read about it as a boy. When the next group left, I was once again alone with my thoughts. I had only ten days left; the time had passed quickly. The owner of the camp was Saad Bing Jung, a prince left over from the Raj. A mahseer fisherman, it was his stretch of the river and he had fished it since being a boy, his best fish having been a monster golden mahseer of 104lb. He fished with a beaten-up old hardy spinning rod with most of the cork missing and lashed up with tape. It matched his character. He'd come into camp a few times over the weeks and as I'd been there we had fished together. He didn't act like a prince, just a fisherman. But just sometimes it came out. One day we fished together, I put in a long cast downstream. I'd been practising. But Saad's cast fell just short. He then wound in and cast again, this time to his guide across the river who picked up his ragi, got into his coracle and took his bait downriver before finally dropping it six feet in front of mine. He then looked at me with a glint in his eyes and chuckled to himself. I had to laugh. Another time he turned up, having learnt it had been my birthday a few days earlier with a birthday cake in one hand and an exquisite silk shirt beautifully wrapped in the other. Of course, it fitted perfectly. The final time he came into camp was on my last night after fishing.

For the last week or so, armed guards accompanied me, carrying loaded assault rifles, as I went off to fish in the jeep. As I fished they looked out for trouble. A notorious bandit had made the news as he was again on the loose; kidnapping foreigners was high on his agenda. I fished on undeterred. On my final evening just before heading off to fish Crocodile Rock a jeep full of soldiers turned up with their leader. He said it was too risky to leave camp which left me feeling gutted. Only the Camp Pool remained. I headed off to fish the Cauvery River for the final time, expecting nothing to happen. I was accompanied by two armed soldiers and guide. I cast out the ragi and sat enjoying my last evening. I became caught in the rocks a couple of times then baited and cast a couple of times. By now it was early evening and as dusk began to fall a night owl flew above. I was thinking of the tree house and the month spent in camp. It had been amazing. Suddenly, and without warning, the rod jarred down hard. I struck and a mahseer bolted off downriver I couldn't believe my luck. It was heading for a shoot, reach it and I knew it would be gone. I piled on the pressure and somehow managed to turn it. I really felt sure I'd lose it. But the guide had by now jumped to his feet and was standing next to me, stringer in hand. The mahseer came close then bolted off again downstream, this time, thankfully, with less power. It was tiring. I coaxed it back and as it came close and passed upstream close by, I could see it was a good fish. "Grab it!" I shouted. The guide was ahead of me and what turned out to be a 40lb silver mahseer was again at my feet on a stringer. We all cheered. My hands were shaking again as weapons were dropped and the trophy shot was taken. It was the icing on the cake.

40lb silver mahseer.

I returned back to camp and when Saad turned up I told him the story. After landing a 104lb golden mahseer himself I knew that to him a 40lb fish was

40lb of silver mahseer close-up.

40lb silver mahseer on a stringer prior to release.

an average size but still he shared my happiness. I left camp the next day. Saad drove me the three-hour ride back to Bangalore and took me to his place. As expected it looked exactly as I imagined, complete with tiger rug on the floor. "Do you want a tea?" he asked.

"No, a beer," I replied and he laughed. After he had left the room I looked to see the photo of the massive fish framed on the wall. I gazed at it in a state of awe. It was huge. He handed me the beer. Then we said our goodbyes and his driver took me first to a local market to buy silk then on to the airport. I flew first to Chennai, taking an overnight stop home. It had been a month I will never forget.

Thursday 25th February 2004.

Fishing this morning, turned myself inside out mentally, was glad to stop fishing. Went to fish at 4.00pm and the police turned up and said I couldn't fish Crocodile Rock only Camp Pool because of the bandits. Fate!

Hooked a big mahseer, couldn't believe it!! One hour of fishing left after a month. Had a hell of a fight just managing to stop it going down the rapids. Landed a 40lb

*silver mahseer. What an amazing end to my time here
and certainly made my trip.*

10.00pm

*Sat alone in the tree house for the last time. Will
I return? I don't know, as I have other fish to catch. It's
not every night you drink beer sat with a prince, catch a
40lb mahseer and sleep in a tree house.*

Three years later I received an e-mail out of the
blue. It was titled quite simply, Subhan. Before I'd
even read it I knew this could only mean one thing -
that he had died. Like so many other fishermen who
had been lucky enough to have fished with him he
had touched me. I felt a great loss.

Subhan.

Chapter 8.

Frazer River, B.C. Canada.

$\mathcal{L}$ had always planned to return to Canada one day. The last visit was in 1999. I flew to Vancouver and stayed in a backpacker's to regain my bearings then headed north, an arduous Greyhound bus journey of twenty one hours to fish the Skeena River for steelhead. On arriving, I found to my horror the weather was bad and the Skeena flooded. I should have checked! I stuck it out for a few days, then fled back to Vancouver and flew onto Caracas Venezuela, bonefishing, my backup plan. It was to be five years before I returned.

I'd come up with a plan. After trying to go it alone it hadn't worked. I needed help and that meant one thing, guides. I had little money but air miles enough for a return flight to Vancouver. I found a flight available in September, a prime time for the giant white sturgeon, which lived in the Frazer River. I booked it in the hope I could find help, someone to share the guide prices. This came in the shape of Nick, a Hampshire solicitor I'd met in camp in India, the guy who had caught the 50lb mahseer. He made the fatal mistake of coming to see me one day. I took him to my office, the local pub, and by the end of our lunchtime drinking session I had roped him in. I was set to return. I knew after my research that September was when the really big sturgeon came and like sharks they hoovered up the spent salmon. There were lots, as the Frazer River carried the most in the world, pink, chum, sockeye, kings and the joy of all Canadian salmon fishermen, coho, the bright leaping bars of silver.

I met Nick at Heathrow; he, like me years ago looked green, although he was older than me I don't think he understood the situation he was in. At that point I'd been roughing it and fishing around the world for the past thirteen years. Like me, he liked women, and I knew the bar below the backpacker's in Vancouver where I planned to stay was full of them. We entered feeling jet-lagged and dumped our gear then went downstairs. Nick seemed impressed with the pub. We both woke blurry eyed; it had been a good night. That day, after checking out the art galleries, we arranged for a taxi to take us the forty miles or so to Mission, a township on the Frazer River. We left after sinking a few beers at the pub. I felt that I'd done my job after weeks of e-mailing, everything had been put into place. I sat back, half cut, and relaxed for the first time in months as it had been so difficult to get here. I gazed out of the window and watched the scenery pass until finally we left Vancouver and entered into the countryside - the white sturgeon were waiting. Nick didn't know what he was in for, I did. We were dropped off at our accommodation, a hotel. We went upstairs and Nick went outside to smoke on the balcony while I followed. "Nick, I'm here for a seven foot fish, what are you after?" I said. He thought I was joking but I assured him I wasn't. I'd been in this situation before, chasing giant fish. I told him there and then as he smoked, he would get one chance and if he messed it up the fish would be gone. "Fight it like you are fighting me!" I told him. "Think when I've beat you up, get back up and hit me to knock me out!" It was the best advice I could have given him. He laughed but didn't take the advice onboard.

The next morning, we peered down below from the balcony. The guide with the four-wheel drive and jet boat was waiting! It was only a short drive. The boat was put in the slip and before we knew it we were speeding up the Frazer River hunting white sturgeon. The Frazer River felt good as the jet boat sped upriver; the weather was calm if a little nippy. I stood on the deck, and clung onto the cabin, feeling free as we raced to fish the first mark. The boat was stopped and the anchor dropped. Soon, rods were baited and cast then put into rod holders. We were fishing at last. The set-up was simple. Multiplier reels on light eight foot rods with braid for main line. Attached to that a small weight and running ledger; the bait, salmon eggs, wrapped in women's tights made into egg-shaped balls lightly hooked to a 6/0 barbless hook. Nick was first up. We watched the four rods with baited breath for the first bite. It wasn't long before one of the rods began to twitch. Nick grabbed the rod and struck. He was into his first sturgeon. It leapt and revealed itself as a small fish of around 30lb or so. While Nick played the 30lber the guide told us the story of a 13ft sturgeon which was caught years before. The Chinese watched eagerly the fight from the Mission bridge. Most of the day was spent bidding for the fish as in those days they were allowed to be killed. Today, happily, all white sturgeon on this mighty river are released, in fact they are protected. Eventually, when the huge creature was landed, it weighed in at over 1000lb. These fish are old time capsules, if they could speak they could surely tell a tale or two. Nick soon had the 30lb sturgeon aboard and I looked at one of these amazing fish for the first time. A chocolate brown back and a cream belly with white diamond marking's down its side, a shark-like tail and it's mouth underslung with feelers enabling it to search out its prey. It was quickly unhooked and released, swimming off strongly down river.

Baby white sturgeon.

After Nick's fish I was up. We moved to a different mark, the anchor was dropped, rods baited and cast. I watched all four rods carefully. Half an hour had passed, one rod twitched. A bite. I carefully took it out of its rod holder feeling the fish move off, then I struck. The rod instantly buckled under the strain and I was into my first sturgeon. It was a good one too. As I played the fish the anchor was pulled.

A good sign! This fish didn't leap, it stayed deep in the depths using its power in the river. Finally, after half an hour, I began to see its tail patterns and got my first sight of it. A good fish at around six feet long. I hung on to the fish as the boat dragged the fish to the shore where, after photos, we sent her on her way. For me it was a very good start.

Releasing a white sturgeon.

Again, the jet boat powered off and Nick was up. Excited, after the six footer, Nick watched the four rods with renewed vigour. It was not long before a rod started to twitch. He slowly took the rod out of its holder and struck hard. The strike didn't allow the rod to fully lift, he was into a monster! We followed that fish for over an hour. Nick moaned and groaned, whilst I fed him water. "I don't now if I want to fight this," he said. My answer was to ask him what the hell he was doing here then. That sturgeon dragged us around with Nick still whingeing about fighting it. I had warned him he would get one chance but the fish dictated the fight and eventually got under a power cable and was lost. It must have been a huge fish as it had acted like it didn't even know it was hooked. We returned to the slip. We were shellshocked as we entered the local bar on the shore; it had been an amazing start to the fishing! As we drank, we reflected on the day's fishing and watched the barmaids who were beautiful. I felt content and I think Nick was too. A long night was to follow, with both of us getting horribly drunk. We woke bleary eyed. The next day we didn't start fishing until 1.00pm. It was good to have a chance to catch our breath and recover from the previous night's drinking. The guide turned up at 12.00pm at the hotel and took us the short ride to the jetty and the waiting jet boat. Gear was quickly loaded onboard, the engine started and again we were soon powering up the Frazer River. Our guide that day was Tom. Like me, Tom was a loner. He had a girlfriend but chose to live alone in a trailer on the banks of the Frazer River close to the fish. I only learnt this after Nick had flown back to England one evening. After his client's left we drank beer together around a fire outside his trailer. Like all good fisherman he was passionate about his fishing and, as the Americans say, would go the extra mile to get what he wanted. He awoke daily at first light to gather fresh bait, eggs from dying chum salmon and their dead skin, stink bait as he called it. With a hangover one morning, one sniff and I had to swallow hard. Hence its name.

That day we both caught sturgeon but only small ones. The best was maybe 60lb. They were still very strong and fought and leapt like freshwater marlin. As evening came and the sun began to set we tied up to another boat, Vic Carroe's, the head guide of the company I had booked the trip with. He was fishing with Ross - another Englishman and sturgeon fisherman - who had caught some huge fish. We dropped lines and sat quietly waiting for a bite. When it came it was on my rod, a twitching tip indicated a bite. I gently picked up the rod from its holder; I could feel the sturgeon mouthing the bait then it moved off, the rod loaded under the pressure and I struck hard, as hard as I could. The rod hardly moved from that moment…we all knew I was into a huge fish. It felt the hook and my back creaked under the strain as it powered off. It was getting dark by now and in the twilight I had to leap onto Vic's boat to try to control it. It had done a monster run this time, back towards the boat. Reeling like a man possessed I again managed to come tight on the fish again, it was under the boat. Then it headed for the surface and leapt. When it did no one else saw it except me as it had leapt at the front of the boat and was hidden by the cabin. "It's huge!" I shouted as it disappeared back into the depths of the river. It looked like a serpent, a sea monster. Now I had seen what I had hooked I was desperate to land it. The boat was untied, anchor buoyed, and Nick jumped aboard as we drifted off into the darkness. Tom shouted out, "Don't forget which boat you hooked it on!" The fight lasted an hour and a half and when the sturgeon finally succumbed the boat dragged it to the shore for the trophy shots. I wouldn't give the rod over until I was sure the sturgeon was beaten. When it was, I leapt overboard and in the shallows near the shore dropped the rod. I pounced on the head of a giant white sturgeon lit up by the flood lights of the boat. It was huge, over 7ft long and Vic estimated it at 350lb. The fight had been unbelievable. Nick put on waders and jumped overboard to help me handle

Frazer River, B.C. Canada.

Bite time on the Frazer River.

Hooked up to a monster white sturgeon.

the fish. In the darkness, I put its massive head on my knee whilst Nick tried to contain its shark-like tail. Vic took the trophy shots from his boat and once I was sure we had a good shot I unhooked the barbless hook from its underslung mouth and it sloped off as though it had just had its daily workout. In the bar that night the beers were, of course, on me.

Tuesday 12th October 2004.

What an amazing days fishing! Started at 1.00pm and fished till around 10.00pm. Just before dark I hooked into a huge sturgeon. What a fight! One of the hardest fights I have ever had with a fish, it was gruelling. When the fish jumped at the front of the boat it was spectacular! We were tied up to another boat and I had to keep leaping from one to another. Finally I leapt on the other boat the engine was started and we chased it! Quite amazing to hook a fish on one boat and chase it on the other it was truly mad. Finally I landed what turned out to be a huge sturgeon of over seven feet long estimated at well over 350lb. A dream come true!

I had brought Nick to Canada for a big fish and except for the monster he had lost all the best sturgeon were falling to my rod. I was desperate for him to land a big fish. That night, in the bar, I told him that the next day all the rods would be his. At first, he refused, but after I insisted he accepted. Of course, I made him pay for the pleasure and we both awoke the next morning worse for wear. All day Nick caught sturgeon but when the day was over he had caught nothing bigger than a 50lb fish. The next day was our final day after the sturgeon, I reassured him that it was not all over until the fat lady sings. I just had a gut feeling it was going to be special. Again, Tom was our guide. The last day was quite staggering; eight fish, none under five and a half feet, and Nick finally landed a big sturgeon of six feet. He left that evening shellshocked as it had been a mad week of fishing. I stayed on to salmon fish my best fish - a Chum of 18lb caught on a fly, but it was to be the white sturgeon of the Frazer River which I will never forget with their power and fighting abilities which put a lot of sportfish to shame. It had been a good trip and I returned home feeling excited. Come January I was once again off to New Zealand to chase the trout of Taupo.

Chapter 9.
Taupo, New Zealand.

As a boy in England I was used to catching trout using worms. So to be fly fishing in Taupo, New Zealand, as a man felt like coming home. After fishing around the world in many places one thing was for sure, trout held memories.

In Taupo there are serious fishermen. Number one is Tom Northcroft, his father's fish of nineteen and a half pounds is in the Taupo museum caught from the Waitahanui Rip back in the hay days of Taupo when the fish were huge. His great friend is Bill Wilson, a canny Scotsman. They are very astute fisherman and don't suffer fools gladly so when they became my friends, I felt as though I was understood for once. Perhaps they may have seen a little of themselves in me. Every time I bumped into them they were surprising. Needless to say, they usually out fished me. Eight years had past since I had first discovered Taupo. I came up with the idea of living in a van, lonely maybe, but it was like my office. I could eat, sleep and dream fish and also have a place in which to tie flies. I'd found a contact in Auckland who could supply me with a Toyota Hiace van for next to nothing. Arriving in Auckland after three days flying made me feel weird but when I saw the van, even in my jet-lagged state I knew the research had paid off. It was perfect. I was handed the keys then fled to Taupo to fish. After three days flying I knew it was crazy to drive but I was so desperate to fish I knew I wouldn't sleep. I arrived in Taupo just as it was getting dark then drove out of the township and ended up at a tiny stream mouth on the shores of Lake Taupo. I was hoping to see Bill but sadly he wasn't there. I could see the line of fishermen in the darkness, but I was so tired I slept, easy in the knowledge I'd come home once again.

My Toyota Hiace van.

I awoke early the next morning. The night fishermen like the night owls had left. I boiled the kettle on the small gas stove in the van and drank a black coffee while watching the lake. I felt excited. I'd planned a four-month trip fishing the rivers and rips of Taupo; it was time to fish.

I drove to Waitahanui to fish the rip where I bumped into Bill. I hadn't seen him for a year. "You're back then and you've put on weight, get fishing." He was right. I was sprawled out in the back of the van half asleep trying to recover from the jet lag. "Are you fishing?" was his next question.

"Of course," I said, and clambered into my waders. He didn't waste any time and was fishing by the time I joined him in the rip. It was good to see him again and as we fished we talked. The New Zealand sun was hot, the rip against my waders cool, it was summer. No fish were caught that day out of the rip but it was still a joy to fish there again. I was back again in Taupo for one thing - a 10lb trout and, as I was fussy, it had to be a fresh rainbow hen. Of course, both Bill and Tom had caught double figure fish but they don't come easy. Only a few fishermen are lucky enough to catch one. They usually come at night out of the darkness from the deep water to feed on the smelt and koura in the many rips formed from rivers and streams which enter the lake. The challenge was set and I was going to do everything in my power to nail one. I knew one thing, I had to put in the time. The next day, I had recovered slightly from my jet lag; it was time to kit out the van. So I drove into Taupo to do the charity shops! The first thing I bought was woollen army blankets then pots and pans all from the Salvation Army. I did splash out on a brand new whistling kettle, bought from Warehouse one of New Zealand's cheapest stores, as I knew it was going to be well used. It took most of the day to kit out the van so afterwards I sat outside one of the local bars drinking a beer or two, basking in the late afternoon sun while watching the lake; I felt I had done well. That night I returned to camp to sleep. Before going to sleep I drank a black coffee whilst listening to my radio. Needless to say, I slept well.

My alarm clock was set for the unearthly hour of 4.00am. When it went off, I was bleary eyed and still jet-lagged and it was all I could manage to crawl out of bed to boil the kettle. It was time to fish. Fishing in Taupo starts at 5.00am and finishes at midnight. The witching hour in the morning is the hour or so before it gets light. After it's fully light the trout return back to the deep after feeding on smelt and koura in the security of darkness. I drank my black coffee before climbing into my waders. I stood there, rod in hand, alone on the shore at a tiny river mouth at 4.50am. At 5.00am I entered the shallows, casting as I went. I was knee deep, casting into the darkness, and rusty as it had been a year since I had fished, but after a while it came back. As I fished I gazed up at the stars, unaccompanied by the moon. They were bright that morning. I watched a shooting star when the fly was seized. It was a vicious take and nearly ripped the fly rod out of my hands. The reel raced and I was into my first fish. I heard the splash out in the lake as it leapt, a fresh fish. It was magic and reminded me of why I was here. When I beached the trout the torch revealed a bright fat silver hen of 4lb. I killed it and buried it in the pumice sand, marking it with a stick. It was my only fish that morning. When the sun was fully up I returned to the van and boiled the kettle then sank another black coffee laced with manuka honey before washing and cleaning the fish in the tiny stream. A shag turned up and made light work of the guts just off the shore. That morning I drove into Taupo for breakfast, dropping off the trout at the local butchers along the way, to be smoked and vacuum packed. I wouldn't kill another until I'd eaten this one. I would pick it up a few days later and wash it down with my beer. There is no better meal for any fisherman! It was still only 9.00am but as I ate and read the Taupo Times I felt good and ready for the day ahead as knew there was no better way to start any day in Taupo.

As the weeks passed I fished my socks off chasing those Taupo trout, any news I heard concerning fish I would take the van and set up camp. Sometimes I would nail them, other times nothing. Mostly I fished in the dark, feeling lonely and at times it was hard going but I knew this was my best chance at a big fish. Of course, all was quickly forgotten when I met a hard fighting fish. When the weather prevented me from fishing, the hours were filled by tying flies in the van overlooking the Waitahanui Rip. It was a good way to pass the time and save money. Tom and Bill would turn up from time to time to keep an eye on me. We talked of the fishing; they kept me going, even smoking me trout. They knew I had little money. I would also bump into other fishermen from all over New Zealand and from all over the world. It was good company, the conversations were always interesting and of course always fishing related.

Fishing at the Waitahanui Rip was always a pleasure, especially when the trout were running.

Summer fishing at the Waitahanui Rip.

Tom Northcroft & Bill Wilson at Waitahanui.

Taupo, New Zealand.

Fresh run brace I caught from the Waitahanui Rip.

Lovely fish, powerful and full of fight. I'd also fish the Tongariro River with dry cicadas, seeing a fish porpoise out of the rapids and hit the fly made the hairs on the back of my neck stand up

Monday March 7th 2005.

Sat in the sun overlooking lake Taupo drinking a beer reflecting on today's fishing. What an amazing day! The first trout I caught today was small but very pretty. The next two were full of fight and extremely powerful, then a lovely bright silver jack all caught on dry cicadas. The biggest was 4lb caught from the Red Hut Pool. I stood mesmerised as it appeared out of the deep green depths, as it did by instinct I crouched down to keep hidden from its field of vision, it enhaled the tiny nymph which I'd hung under the dry fly. Truely mind blowing stuff. The two fisherman watching from the Red Hut Bridge above had saw the whole story unfold and yelled as I'd hooked it! A perfect long cast into Waddells Pool under a bush made another fish crash the dry cicada. I had her as well a hen of 3lb. The

Duchess Pool produced another small fish of a 1lb which leapt everywhere and to finish off a wonderful day I managed to hook a hard fighting fresh run bright silver jack of 3lb which must have ran up the river in the rain we had last night, it really was trout fishing at its very best. An incredible day. All fish I released.

Tongariro trout gets released.

Cicada.

When the cicada's disappeared and the summer was over I stuck to fishing the rips in hope of that big fish. The weather was starting to turn cold, bitter at times, especially in the mornings with the wind chill coming off the mountains. It was April and I knew after my research that this month along with May is prime time for those big fish to come in. When conditions were right on moonless nights, fishermen would gather. Bill and I fished together most nights and Tom would usually be about. It was always good to fish with them.

The fish were putting on weight and getting back into condition. Having fished every day for the last two months I could watch it all happen. When my big fish did come it was at Hatepe Rip and of course, Bill and Tom had a part in it. I caught it on a fly pattern designed by Tom which I had copied. That night, Tom wasn't there but Bill was, being a left hander he was able to fish close to me. The rips change constantly in Taupo due to the wind flows, levels of the lake, etc. The rip that night had been split into three, each going in different directions. We had fished the change of light with no takes but half an hour into the darkness Bill was into his first fish and it was a good one. After he beached that in short succession he hooked and landed another two. I hadn't had even so much as a take and as I said, I was standing right beside him. Before he left he told me to stand where he had been. He pointed out to me a small drop off, I could feel it in the pumice under my feet. Bill had long gone and with not even a touch I was at the point where I thought I'd give it another half an hour before I'd stop for the night. I cast out into the darkness, a long cast, as far as I could, and began to retrieve. The fly was hit hard and as soon as it was I knew I was into a big fish. I heard the splash a long way out as it leapt. It came out of the darkness, leaping constantly back towards me. I knew it was a hen. I wound like mad trying to keep tight on the fish but it was out of control. For a split second, the line went slack and I thought she was gone but much to my relief everything tightened again as she turned and made a monster run straight out into the lake. I switched on my head torch to look at the reel; the fly line had disappeared and I was deep into the backing. She wasn't stopping. I had to do something so I piled on as much pressure as the rod would take; luckily I managed to stop her. Again she turned. I began backing to the shore, she had stopped leaping and I could now feel her weight as she swam. My headlight was off now as knew I dare not scare her or I'd surely lose her. I finally made it to the shore and with one final effort I dragged her up on the pumice. I dropped the rod and pounced on the fish. When I turned the torch on my eyes nearly popped out my of head - it was huge, a hen and as fat as any trout I've ever seen. Later I measured her to find she was 23 inches long to the fork of her tail and weighed 9lb (a condition factor of over 70). It wasn't the 10ber but thought that would do! My hands were shaking. I put the fish in the van and drove back to camp. It was late. I still had one thing to do, get my trophy shot. I set up the camera in the darkness on a self-timer and got the shots. When I eventually climbed into bed I gazed at the fish on the tiny screen of my digital camera. Wow, what a fish, was what I thought as I drifted off to sleep. The next morning I took the fish into the best smokehouse in Turangi where it was smoked and vacuum packed into small individual pieces. As it was such a special fish, I had to do it justice. I returned back to England with the fish at the end of May and handed out the pieces to my family. Sitting in the Airstream, eating the trout along with Somerset cider, was lovely. I knew one thing for sure - fishing Lake Taupo's rips at night had hooked me and I knew that one day I would return.

9lb Taupo hen rainbow trout.

Chapter 10.
Return to Los Roques.

$\mathcal{L}$ just had to return to Venezuela to chase bonefish again. My chance came as I was sitting in the local bar in 2006 in Turangi (New Zealand) after a day's dry fly fishing on the Tongariro River. James was an Aussie who built factories; Jo his soul mate. I'd met them a year earlier. They asked me where I went bonefishing. "That information is for my wife," I replied.

"You said you were never getting married," was James's reply. "Exactly," I said.

After I had returned to the UK I e-mailed James and propositioned him. "If you pay for the guides I will take you bonefishing, and show you the ropes," I said. To my surprise he agreed.

"Where are we going?" asked James.

"Los Roques Venezuela," was my answer. At once I went to work e-mailing all my contacts and setting up the trip. James and Jo were coming to the UK anyway to catch up with friends and family so everything fitted together perfectly. We made a date to meet in Somerset at my place and for me to take them to a notorious cider farm. James and Jo turned up a couple of months later. He rang me on his mobile outside the local pub, unlike me he liked phones! I told them to stay there then I left on my Honda NX650 motorcycle to find them. When I found them they both looked the same if a little shellshocked. I kept my helmet on and they followed me back to my office, the Airstream. When we arrived I took my helmet off, hugged Jo and shook hands with James. It was good to see them again. I'd worked out some local accommodation for them - a bed and breakfast on a farm just up the road. Jo drove whilst me and James caught up. Like Nick, he was older than me but not in fishing years. I think James realised that. Before taking them to the cider farm. I took them to Heavens Gate on Lord Baths estate, Longleat. I wanted them to see the sculptures my brother Paul had carved.

Paul's sculptures.

When James and Jo saw them they didn't say much; as sometimes words are not needed. We had talked about them in the bar in Turangi after a days fishing. We left and I took them to the cider farm. James cringed every time he took a mouthful but I knew he would drink it, as if he bought cheese it was free. We drove back, with him complaining it wasn't so strong, so I asked him why. He had talked to the guy who put the apples in the press, a complete stranger for over an hour. Being from Somerset, I'd done it to a few. They dropped me off back at the Airstream and I arranged to meet them both ten days later in London. I kissed Jo on the cheek, shook James's hand and they left.

With everything put in place ten days later as arranged I arrived in London to meet them. I'd had a problem getting there so I arrived late. As I checked into the airport hotel, I met James and Jo coming down the stairs. James, being an Aussie, gave me grief. I dumped my bags in the room and we left for the nearest pub to catch up. We all roomed together that night to save on costs. When morning came, James and I left for Heathrow early to fly to Caracas but Jo wasn't going. James kissed her goodbye and arranged to meet her two weeks later in Miami.

We were on different flights but as arranged I

landed first. In the chaos of Caracas airport I waited for James's flight to come in. He turned up an hour or so later. It felt like it had been a long journey to get to this point in my life. It had been nearly ten years since I first arrived here. Now I was showing someone else the ropes. We grabbed a taxi and we left for a local hotel, a thirty minute drive down the coast.

The next day we returned to the airport where we exchanged our US dollars for Bolivar, the local currency. The touts gave us a good exchange rate on the black market. In the domestic terminal for the flight to Los Roques, it was, as ever, chaotic, made worse by my broken Spanish. Eventually though we boarded the aircraft for the forty minute flight to Grande Roque. When we took off I just hoped the guide would be waiting at the other end. I gazed out of the window and noticed the sea was looking flat. I felt excited. I waited to catch the first glimpse of the islands. As they started to appear, I watched James looking on in wonder as he took photos. He said nothing. The plane flew over Grande Roque then circled before landing. I was back. As we left the aircraft James smiled and said, "So this is Los Roques." Like me, he knew the bonefish were waiting.

I walked across the tarmac and spotted our guide. It was a relief, and I knew from that moment things were going to work out okay. The guide took us to our accommodation, a simple posada close to the shore. It was late evening by the time we had settled in. We dumped our gear and left for the local bar, it was time for a beer.

I was up early, first light. James was still asleep while the island and it's fishermen were just waking up in tune with the fish. I sat alone in the twilight in the sand, propped up by one of the local's fishing boats. I sat overlooking the ocean, watching tarpon roll and feed in between the boats. When the sun was fully up I returned to the posada, by now James was awake. I smothered myself from head to foot in suncream before having my breakfast. Then I set up my rods, it was time to fish. The guide turned up on time and we took a short walk down the shore, where we were met by the waiting boat and boatman. Soon we were off. I dangled my hand in the water. It felt cool, the sea gin-clear, you could see the bottom; the air was balmy, it felt like heaven. I was excited to be back again and once more chasing bonefish.

We left the turquoise shallow water, the bottom disappeared and the sea became aqua marine. After crossing the channel the engine was cut, the boat stopped and we jumped out to fish our first flat. I told the guide to stick with James. They went in one direction, I went in the other. I watched the guide and James as they waded; then, thirty metres or so in front of me, I saw bonefish and they were coming my way. I made ready and when they came into casting distance I cast, the fly landed just in front of them, it was a huge school. I stripped the fly back, my heart in my mouth, nothing! I quickly cast again and this time the fly stopped. I struck. A fish! It bolted off scattering the school. I was hard fast into my first bonefish. As I played the fish I could see James and the guide watching the school, which was now heading their way. The guide pointed, James cast a couple of times, and then James too was into a fish, his first ever bonefish. I had landed my fish by now and slowly made my way over to James to watch the fight and get a photograph. That day we landed five bonefish each, all around 4lb, it had been a good start.

Over the next five days we caught over fifty bonefish between us. The highlight for me was watching James hook a bonefish in shallow water. We were wading a huge flat far out in the lagoon near to the shore. A sandy bottom, the water only knee-deep, gin clear, as we waded the warm

5lb bonefish.

Underwater bonefish.

seawater glistening in the afternoon sun. James and the guide stalked the flat close to shore while I stalked the outside. Then they came, out of the blue, a school of five bonefish. I watched on in wonder as they hugged the shoreline using the cover, but the guide, like me, had spotted them and he pointed them out to James. He made ready to cast and when he was in range he dropped the fly just in front of the school. Again I looked on as the lead fish saw the fly then sped up. James stripped the fly back, the fish was on it and excited and instantly pounced on it. He struck and it raced off with James attached, his fly rod high above his head, the school scattering as the bonefish raced off down the flat. This was all happening in front of my very own eyes, it was magic.

As well as bonefish that week we also caught spanish mackerel, bonito, tuna, blue runner, tarpon, barracuda, yellowtail as well as horse-eyed jack. We even cast at permit. It was late October, the tides were high, so most bonefish were caught in the deeper water. But there was to be a bonus: tarpon at this time of year were here in numbers and the prospect made me tingle with excitement.

James was first up. The guide looked at my vast selection of tarpon flies and much to my delight picked the only two I had tyed! We sped off to a huge area - a flat, as far as the eye could see - the engine was cut and we were poled along near to the mangroves. "Everyone look in different directions," I said. We all scanned the huge flat in search of any signs of fish. It was not until a half an hour had passed that I spotted them. "There," I said and pointed to a small school of four fish. They were following the shoreline near the mangroves. The guide got us close in. "Cast, James!" I shouted. He was on the front of the boat the first shot was no good. Again he loaded up the fly rod and cast the fly. It dropped perfectly, just in front of the school. He let it sink and began to strip the fly back. The lead fish followed the fly, sped up opened its mouth and James nailed it. Immediately we all shouted as a tarpon of 35lb was hooked and instantly took to the air.

James had come a long way since I first met him two years previously in Taupo. I kept bumping into him and his girlfriend Jo. One day, wandering around Taupo, I met them in the street and told them I was living in a caravan on the lake front. I found out they were leaving soon so I invited them round for a beer. We said our goodbyes and went our separate ways. I didn't expect to see them again.

I was sitting outside the caravan in the evening sun one afternoon, half cut. I heard a vehicle approaching and it stopped. "Hello!" someone shouted. The voice sounded familiar. It was James and Jo. It was quite unexpected and had come totally out of the blue. They came into the caravan where I handed James a beer, I knew he felt at home. Before he drank most of my beer that evening I took both of them to the shore and gave them casting instruction. I could see that they had both taken it on board. They were leaving the next day so again we said our goodbyes.

The next year I again managed to return to Taupo. I went to see Alan, a mate, a fisherman and a fly tyer, in Barry Greigs, a Turangi fly fishing shop. He had taught me a lot over the years. He laughed when I entered the shop and his first words were, "The Aussies are back, said if you showed up they would like to meet you." I bought flies and told him to tell them to meet me in the pub at 3.00pm after I'd finished fishing. Later I walked up to the car park to enter the bar. James and Jo came out to greet me we shook hands then went inside for a beer (Waikato). That afternoon we all fished together on the Tongariro River. I watched James fish; his casting had improved dramatically. "Christ James", I said,

"Your casting's improved."

He replied, "I just listened to what you taught me last year." It felt good to get some recognition for a change.

After the trophy shots, James unhooked the tarpon and it swam off strongly. The boat was started and we raced off. James was grinning from ear to ear; he had caught it on his nine weight.

35lb tarpon nears the boat.

I was even happier as I knew I was next up for a shot at a tarpon. The following morning after a thirty minute ride across the flats the engine was cut. In the six foot deep crystal clear water we could see a small area of seagrass full of baitfish and tarpon. They looked huge and patrolled between the baitfish carving lines between them. I stood on the front of the boat rod in hand waiting for a shot. What happened next is best described by this diary entry.

Monday 23rd October 2006.

The day, as ever, started early. Three spanish mackerel to start. We then moved on and caught bonefish in the muddy water. James spotted a shoal of fish; the guide cast and hooked a horse-eyed jack. James was handed the rod and fought the fish, a dogged fight, and a fish of 10lb or so.

I cast a few times with a light spinning rod and a large barracuda smashed the lure on the surface. It was hooked and went nuts, out of control crashing across the flats with me hung on. Finally I landed what turned out to be a 30lber.

Next I was up for a chance at hooking a tarpon on the fly. We moved to a flat with a shoal of baitfish on. Instantly we began to spot fish, tarpon and they were

30lb barracuda.

huge. I cast a few times, nothing. Then came three huge fish. I cast at them, one peeled off from the other two, chased the fly and sped up, my heart was in my mouth. Its huge mouth opened and engulfed the fly. I struck! The power as it felt the hook was unreal, instantly leaping all across the flats, going crazy, its armoury of silver scales lighting up in the sun. After the initial hook up the fish swam off like it didn't even know it was hooked. Then it ran! Off the flats and into the deep, the rod creaking under the strain. How could I land such a big fish on a nine weight bonefish rod! I knew it was huge but as I fought it realised it was even bigger than I had first thought! I fought that fish, I gave it everything I know, but still it changed direction and was doing everything in its power for its freedom. The fight continued. Every time I got the fly line back on the reel slowly and surely the tarpon would take line back, it was

Fighting a 40kg tarpon on my nine weight.

turning into a mammoth battle. The fight continued for another forty minutes until the tarpon came to the surface and took air. Thirty minutes then passed with me sweating and being fed water, the tarpon came up again and we all saw the width of its back. "forty kilo," said the guide. Its back had given away its size. Now knowing what I had hooked I knew it would be special if I landed it. Constant fighting against a fish as big as me using inadequate gear was taking its toll. I was aching all over. The guide was hung onto my shorts to stop me going overboard, an hour had now passed. I was winning; the tarpon was tiring, I just couldn't get the final few feet. Just when I thought the tarpon was mine it began to run again. An hour and a half had passed since I first hooked it. The run was unstoppable, the fly line and backing once again disappeared. My heart sank as I knew it wasn't mine. A very clever fish, it had done everything in its power to beat me, which finally it did. It found a coral reef then sped to the surface, leapt and gained its freedom, and as it leapt showing its true beauty before snapping the line. Somehow I didn't feel upset as the whole experience was amazing. The take, the leaping and the fight all happening in front of my eyes had been unbelievable. To finish off a wonderful day I caught a 15lb tuna, which smashed a popper on the surface just off Grande Roque. We both returned home happy, with me aching all over.

Determination, single mindedness and guts have got me all these giant fish as I have never had much money or ever wanted it. One thing is for certain: all my best memories are of fishing and if my time was allotted again I would do it all over again, as I live to fish!

Every man's life ends the same way. It is only the details of how he lived and how he died that distinguishes one man from another.

Ernest Hemingway.

Places Fished.

1993 - Gambia, Giant Threadfin
1994 - Egypt, Nile Perch, Tigerfish
1995 - Zimbabwe, Tigerfish, Vundu Catfish
1995 - Kenya, Sailfish, Marlin
1996 - India, Mahseer
1996 - Madeira, Marlin
1996 - Kenya, Sailfish, Marlin
1997 - Australia, Giant Travelly
1997 - New Zealand, Brown Trout, Rainbow Trout
1998 - Venezuela, Bonefish
1999 - Florida Keys, Tarpon
1999 - Belize, Tarpon, Bonefish
1999 - Venezuela, Bonefish
1999 - Christmas Island, Bonefish
1999 - Belize, Tarpon
2000 - Canada, Steelhead
2000 - Venezuela, Bonefish
2001 - Venezuela, Bonefish
2002 - Australia, Brown Trout
2002 - New Zealand, Brown Trout, Rainbow Trout
2002 - Honduros, Bonefish
2003 - Venezuela, Bonefish, Payara
2004 - India, Mahseer
2004 - Canada, White Sturgeon, Salmon
2005 - New Zealand, Brown Trout, Rainbow Trout
2006 - New Zealand, Brown Trout, Rainbow Trout
2006 - Venezuela, Bonefish, Tarpon
2007 - New Zealand, Brown Trout, Rainbow Trout
2008 - Venezuela, Bonefish
2009 - New Zealand, Brown Trout, Rainbow Trout

The rush of a mahseer,
The leap of a trout,
The attack of a marlin,
The beauty of a bonefish,
The size of a sturgeon,
And the strangeness of a payara.
That is why fisherman fish.